Pr

"From helicopt[illegible] a fast paced adventure. Young adults will love Tibetan Adventure, and so will their parents. Tibetan Adventure is the first book in the adventure travel series Jack L. Parker is writing. I can't wait to read the next one." **James A. Yarrow, MD**

"Dynamite! Jack L. Parker has managed to intricately weave several compelling story lines into a mosaic that retains relevancy and balance. The digression of each thread adds to the aura of the book without deviating from the primary thread." **Robert L. Cabanya**, President, Encruyption Solutions, Inc., Former Marine/Navy Fighter Pilot

"Writer Jack L. Parker leads the reader through a high-altitude adventure in the majestic Himalayas and the beautiful hidden valleys of Tibet. Join Jeff Thornton as he searches for his parents, who are held captive by a power-hungry Chinese colonel. Learn to rely on Dorje, the college-educated guide who fights the communist invaders with his intellect and physical skills. Marvel at the physical beauty of a world seldom visited by Western eyes. This is a tale of beauty, perseverance, and courage fueled by a son's loyalty to his parents. Become a part of the Tibetan Adventure." **Kelvin Lee**, Ed.D School District Superintendent

"*Tibetan Adventure* is a must read for those seeking more than just a story. Author Jack L. Parker masterfully weaves a compelling and exciting tale of friendship, intrigue, and adventure in a setting little known to the Western world." **Greg Nau**

"*Tibetan Adventure* was a thrill for me to read. There were many unexpected twists and turns in the story. My interest was piqued around every corner, and I anticipated adventure. Mr. Parker captured the essence of the country, people, and the scenery in depth This story will intrigue people of all ages." **Cheryl Small**, Cultural Arts Commissioner for the City of Roseville, CA.

"The *Tibetan Adventure*, by Jack L. Parker, is a fast paced story that keeps the reader eager to discover what will happen next to Jeff Thornton as he travels from the comforts of his home in the United States to secret parts of Tibet, a country of both desolation and beauty. Teenagers and adults alike will enjoy reading this book." **Peter W. Gissing,** Colonel, USAF (retired)

"Youth should never be underestimated, as demonstrated by Jeff Thornton. Upon joining forces with an isolated, secret Tibetan tribal community, Jeff plays a key roll in the dangerous and heroic rescue mission of his parents. All of the senses are affected and will keep you electrified to the end. *Tibetan Adventure* is a book for all ages and both sexes." **Linda Bartlett**

tibetan adventure

Jack L. Parker

Tate Publishing & *Enterprises*

This title is also available as a Tate Out Loud audio product.
Visit www.tatepublishing.com for more information.

Cover design by Lynly Taylor
Interior design by Lauren Weatherholt

Published in the United States of America

ISBN: 1-5988655-1-X
07.04.11

This book is dedicated to my wife, Susan, and the many friends who have made this wonderful life even more so.

chapter 1

Jeff Thornton woke from his fitful sleep. It was bitterly cold, and the night was as black as the blackest night can be. The cave in which he and the others sought shelter offered only the barest refuge from the howling wind and blowing snow. Unable to go back to sleep, Jeff tried to let his mind concentrate in hope his thoughts would overcome his feelings of misery and utter futility. Finally, his concentrating was working, and his teeth almost stopped their chattering. With all his will, he forced himself to think only of the events that had caused him to be where he was now. The periodic blasts of icy wind made this more difficult as it roared through the cave, along with the movement of those sharing the cave and his plight. All were huddled, lying as close as possible to each other in their attempt to keep from freezing. Even the hardy Tibetans were having a hard time. He was really thankful for Dorje, his new Tibetan friend. Jeff knew that if it were not for him, he would stand no chance at accomplishing the difficult task that lay before them. It had been a long, rugged trek, and it was not going to get any easier.

"What the heck," he thought proudly to himself. "If I had to do it all again, I would."

Now he felt better, and his thoughts drifted back home to that blustery day in early February.

Something was different. His mother always called out to him when he walked through the front door, especially since she was home on leave of absence from the lab where she worked. Both his parents had been research scientists. However, his dad was presumed dead . . . killed in a plane crash in the Himalayan Mountains while on a scientific research expedition. That was almost a year ago. This was the reason his mother took time off from her work. It was rough on her, but she never complained. She never felt sorry for herself.

Jeff and his dad had drifted apart during Jeff's last two years of high school. Both his parents were working long hours on a special project of some kind. They never discussed this project at home, although he remembered walking into the living room once when they must have been arguing. The only words he heard were, "I will not go through with this terrible thing," spoken by his mother. They said nothing else. He could tell, however, that all was not normal between them. She told him later that the reason his dad went to the Himalayas was to search for a certain kind of plant they needed for their experiments.

During those last two years of high school, Jeff had truly let his grades slide. They slid so far that there was some talk by his teachers that he might not graduate. Normally, Jeff was a very good student who always worked hard in school. No one could understand why he was sloughing off. It was not like him at all, and not even he understood why. He did manage to graduate, but just barely. He guessed it had been the death of his dad that changed his mind about college. He could not get into a four-year college or university, not with his grades, so he had enrolled as soon as he graduated in the local two-year junior college. Throughout his summer courses and the fall semester, he worked hard trying to bring his grades up. He very much wanted to go to a four-year school when he finished junior college.

It wasn't only the quiet of the house that struck him as different. As his eyes became adjusted to the dimness of the room, he let out a yelp. The room was in shambles. It was not only that room, but every room in the house. It looked like a tornado had struck. Even his room, which was normally not the tidiest, had not been spared. Not only was Jeff puzzled, he was afraid. No . . . he was terrified.

"What is going on? What is going on?" he kept saying to himself as he paced up and down the cluttered living room. It was at that instant the doorbell rang. It was a messenger with a special delivery letter addressed to him. Puzzled, he nervously tore open the envelope. Neatly written in longhand, on a plain white sheet of paper, was the following short, direct note:

"Do not panic! I now have both your mother and father. Do not call the authorities! If you do as we instruct, no harm will come to them! Another letter will follow in a few days. Meanwhile, carry on as normal."

Jeff sat heavily on the nearest chair. Now he was really puzzled. The letter said they had both his parents, but his dad was presumed dead.

"Could he," he thought hopefully, "still be alive? Or, was this some kind of sad, sick joke?" He had to admit to himself that he was afraid, confused, and did not know what to do next.

How long he sat there he did not know. Finally, he came to the decision he would not call the police. As the letter said, he would try to carry on as normal. The first thing he did was to put the house back into some kind of order. That took much longer than he expected. It was nearly midnight, and he realized that he was hungry. As he sat eating a sandwich, a plan began to form in his mind.

It was over a week, and Jeff had still not received a second letter. He and his lifelong neighbor and closest friend, Trudy Garrison, sat in his father's den, doing homework. He felt he had finally convinced her that his mother went to visit his aunt. But then Trudy was not just your average teenager. She seemed to have a sixth sense.

Her parents were world travelers. Her father was, in fact, a well-known travel writer, and her mother was a photographer. Trudy had been to more countries by the time she was fifteen than she had fingers and toes. She was hardly ever home during the summer months. Her parents always took her with them when she was out of school on summer vacation. There had even been those times when they took her out of school. Trudy never minded this. She was a fine student and always did the work her teachers gave her when she was traveling during the school year. Besides, her parents felt that travel was a form of education in itself.

Trudy had stuck with and believed in him during those last two lousy years in high school; the years that had almost been his downfall. He realized that it was not only the news of his father's death that straightened him out, but Trudy and his mother, as well. He knew they had always been close. He found out later that they spent many hours trying to find some way for him to come to his senses. He always felt, for some reason, that he and Trudy were always competing, though they were so close. How stupid he had been.

Jeff had always been a bit on the chubby side. Not fat, mind you, but he always looked like he could lose a few pounds, and he was rather clumsy to boot. He was certainly not what you would call athletic. Due to his slight chubbiness, he always looked younger than he really was. Even when he was over six feet tall, people thought he was just tall for his age. That alone was enough to mortify any male in his teens.

In those times when he felt life was at its lowest, he would always go to the little river not far from town. It never seemed to let him down. It was always there, always moving; smooth in one spot, rough in another . . . but it always kept moving. The river seemed to have a purpose. It may be going somewhere, and it had a goal. The river was a lot like life. There were the rough times and the smooth times. The river was wise. It knew where it was going and how to get there with the least amount of effort. How he used to envy the little river. There was a time in his life when he felt he had no purpose. Life seemed so complicated. Why couldn't it be just like the river?

One day as he walked along its banks, his young life at its lowest ebb, he had a sudden urge to join the river; to submerge all of his feelings within its depths. Just as he was about to carry out this urge, the river seemed to speak to him. It seemed to tell him that all would be okay; that he was young and had a whole lifetime ahead, and that life was what you made of it. If you wanted a full, rewarding life, you had to work for it. Nothing came easy. That was when he decided to stop feeling sorry for himself. He would make something of his life and would make those who knew and cared for him proud. He just simply decided to get off his duff and to get back to the real world and face reality.

An extra sharp blast of cold air sliced through the cave, bouncing off the walls. Jeff shivered even more. The Tibetans groaned in their sleep. Finally, he was able to regain his train of thought.

He flashed back to the time when his plan first came to mind. He would begin an exercise program, he told himself. He was determined to put himself not only in good physical condition, but top mental condition, as well.

It turned out to be several weeks before Jeff received the next letter. He was on a diet and was following a strict exercise program.

He was well on his way to being in the best shape of his life, and he felt good. What once had been a rather flabby Jeff was beginning to turn into a lean, muscular Jeff. He knew he still had a long way to go, but he knew he could do it.

Jeff tried unsuccessfully to control his trembling hands as he tore at the flap of the heavily sealed envelope. He jumped at least a foot high when the front doorbell rang. It was Trudy.

"What's in your hand? A letter from a girl," she half-seriously kidded. Immediately she realized something was wrong, so she apologized.

"That's okay," replied Jeff with a quiver in his voice. "It's just that . . . well. A few minutes ago I got this letter, and I'm afraid to open it."

"Why?"

"Because I don't know if what it says is going to be good or bad," he declared. He made a strong effort and finally tore it open. His face turned ashen as he silently began to read. He sat slumped on the couch.

Trudy fidgeted as she watched the movement of his lips as he read. She had felt all along something was wrong, and now she was sure of it.

After he finished reading the letter, Jeff just sat as though in a daze. Finally, he shook himself, sat straight, and looked Trudy in the eye. "I guess," he began in a low, earnest tone, "it's about time I told you just what has been going on." He knew he could trust her; therefore, he did not even dwell on the subject of secrecy. When he was finished telling his bazaar tale, he added the part about this being the reason for his trying to get into shape. It was part of his plan. He had to be prepared for whatever might lie ahead. Yet, until getting this second letter, he was not even sure just what his plan would be. Now he was sure.

Trudy took the letter when Jeff handed it to her, and she read it aloud.

"I do have both your parents. No harm will come to them providing they do as they are told and they will eventually be returned to you.

You will not hear from me again for some time. Carry on just as you have been, or else."

Just as Trudy finished reading the second letter, the doorbell rang, causing both of them to jump. Jeff tiptoed to the door and very carefully opened it just a crack. A man with Asian features stood looking at him. Cautiously, Jeff asked what he wanted.

His only reply was, "Read this." He held out his hand with an envelope in it. When Jeff gingerly took it, the stranger turned and walked quickly off into the night.

"Two letters in one night," Jeff stated as he opened the envelope. "I wonder what will be next."

He read the letter aloud.

"We are your friends. We know who is holding your parents prisoner and where they are being held. We may be able to help you, but you must do as we ask. Tomorrow night at 9 p.m., be at the front entrance to the college library. You will be contacted. Come alone."

"Wow," uttered Jeff. "This means that both my parents are probably alive. I can hardly believe it."

"That's wonderful," exclaimed Trudy in an excited voice.

"Are you going to do as the letter said?" she questioned.

"You bet," was Jeff's firm reply.

"Well, then, I'm going with you."

"Oh, no you're not! I don't want to take any chances. The letter said come alone, and that's just what I'm going to do—that's that!"

"Okay! Okay! I guess you're right for once, anyway," she replied meekly.

chapter 2

A few late stragglers were just leaving the closing library when Jeff arrived at the front door. He waited beneath the single light. It was just after he heard the door lock from the inside that a lone figure approached from some nearby bushes.

"Jeff Thornton?"

"Yes, that's me," came Jeff's hesitant reply.

"My name is Dorje Tsiering. I come to you as a friend. I am here to talk about your parents."

In the dim light, Jeff could just make out the person calling himself Dorje Tsiering. He looked to have sharp, handsome Asian features, and he was tall . . . very tall. Though he spoke with an accent, his English was very good. For some unknown reason, Jeff had the feeling he could trust this man. At the suggestion of the stranger, they began to walk. As they walked, Dorje—as he asked Jeff to call him—would often look back over his shoulder. Jeff asked him why.

"One never knows if he is being followed. I did take precautions, but as I said, one never knows."

They walked in silence for some time, each trying to get a feel for the other. Finally, Dorje began to speak.

"What I am about to tell you," he began seriously, "may sound like the script from some adventure movie, but I assure you that every word is true. We know that both your parents are research scientists. We also know they were working on a project so secret that one did not know exactly what phase of the project the other was working on. The work they were doing had to do with some kind of chemical warfare. We also know," he continued, "that the person responsible for holding your parents prisoner is trying to force them to finish their research so that he will have the formula. The only way he could achieve this goal is by kidnapping them. I know this may all sound like a pack of lies, but you must believe me."

"Okay, can you tell me just who you are," questioned Jeff, "and why you are so interested in all of this and . . . just where are my parents, anyway?"

"One thing at a time," Dorje replied with a chuckle. "I am from Tibet. My people are Khambans. The Khambans are feared by the regular Tibetans because they are bandits and very independent.

"They answer to no one. They are fierce fighters. If they respect you, they are the truest of friends. When the Chinese invaded my country in 1959, it was the Khambans who fought them the hardest. Even today, my people are still waging war against the Chinese. Now, however, it is a guerrilla kind of warfare. When I was very young, my parents sent me to relatives in Nepal. That is where I went to school, and that is where I learned to speak English. From there, I went on to study at a university in England. Since finishing my studies, I have spent a great deal of time in various countries trying to, and sometimes getting help of various kinds for Tibet."

"But what has all of this to do with me and my parents?" interrupted Jeff.

"I will get to that shortly," replied Dorje patiently. "As I told you, I have been formally educated, which is very rare in my country. After the university, I returned to Tibet to be trained by my people to fight against the Chinese. With my education, they felt I could do more good in the outside world. I now live here in your country. My real job is still to try to get help, in any way I can, for the fight against the Chinese. As a front, I conduct tours, mostly to Nepal. It works out very well.

"Now, to answer your last question, I have had word that they are holding your parents in an ancient monastery in a very remote valley in Tibet."

"But who is holding them? Please, tell me," pleaded Jeff.

"A faction of the Chinese army," answered Dorje. "They are a secret society within the army and have a rather large membership. Their goal is eventually to gain control of the entire Chinese army. Control of the army means control of China. We have sound reason to believe that they have kidnaped your parents so they can force them to make this weapon for them. It is a chemical so terrible that in the wrong hands, it could mean that even the most powerful nations would have to give in to their demands. They are ruthless and would stop at nothing to get what they want. Their leader is the most ruthless of all. He is a colonel, and his name is Chew Chin. He is from an old, very powerful and rich Chinese family. He went to military college in Russia and is truly a fiend."

This last statement caused Jeff's whole body to shudder. They said nothing more for a few minutes. Dorje wanted to give some time for what he had just told Jeff to sink into his head.

"All right," began Jeff, breaking the silence, "now that you have answered my questions and I think you are on the up and up, what do you want or expect of me?"

"Nothing," was Dorje's firm reply. "I was told to tell you to do nothing. It was felt that you should know about your parents, and we hoped you could be trusted. An attempt is going to be made to try to free them. I cannot say for certain when, but it won't be too far into the future. They have to be set free before Colonel Chin can force them to finish their experiments. If he can carry out his evil wishes . . . well, I don't even want to try to think of how terrible it would be."

"But you don't know my parents. They would never do anything like that."

"Oh, to be sure," Dorje answered sympathetically. "I know that under ordinary circumstances that would be true. But you do not know or realize the terrible means this man would use to make them carry out his wishes."

When Dorje finished his last statement, Jeff's stomach immediately felt like it was tied up in knots. Gritting his teeth, he told Dorje if there was going to be any kind of attempt to free his parents, he was going to be a part of it.

The more Dorje argued against Jeff taking part in the plan, the more stubborn Jeff became. One way or another, he was going to be involved.

At last Dorje agreed to talk to his friends and promised to get back to him just as soon as he got any kind of word. This time, though, instead of sending a note, Dorje said he would call. He would say he was one of Jeff's professors and needed to talk to him about a special assignment he had in mind for him. The reason for the cloak and dagger stuff, Dorje said, was because there was the possibility that they had bugged Jeff's phone. It might also look suspicious if another letter were delivered to his house because they were possibly keeping it under surveillance.

"We will meet as before at the front entrance to the library," Dorje instructed.

They shook hands and parted, each going his own way.

Trudy was anxiously waiting in the living room when Jeff walked in. Immediately, she started throwing questions at him.

"Hold on, hold on for just a minute," he said. "I'll tell you everything that happened, but give me just a little time to get my head together."

He began at the beginning, telling Trudy everything. When he was finished, she sat as though in a trance. It was after several silent minutes when finally she asked in a low, serious tone just what he was planning to do.

Heaving a big sigh, he answered in a matter-of-fact way that one way or another he planned to play a part in freeing his parents. What that part would be, he did not know, but he was determined to be involved whether they gave him the okay or not.

"But Tibet is a big country," Trudy stated. "I do know something about it, you know. You do remember that I went with my parents to Nepal the summer before last on that walking tour—which, by the way, is the only way you can get to Tibet. That is unless you have the permission of the Chinese government, in which case then you can go by road or plane. However, I sincerely doubt that that will be the case. Believe me, it is no easy stroll. Plus, if you tried to do something on your own, just how would you go about finding where your parents are being held? No, you have to face the facts, Jeff. The only way you can go is if these people say it's all right for you to be involved."

"You're right," Jeff replied meekly. "I guess I was not really thinking straight. I just want my mom and dad to come home safe and sound. I certainly do not want the creeps who are holding them prisoners to get the completed formula. The only way to do this is to free them just as soon as possible."

chapter 3

The very next day was Friday, and after their last class, Jeff and Trudy went to the college and public libraries. They checked out everything they could find about Tibet.

After dinner, Trudy came over as usual to do homework. Along with her books, she carried a large brown package. She told Jeff she had found it on his front porch. The package contained a large assortment of material on Tibet, as well as Nepal.

A short unsigned note read, "Study and learn all you can. It is important." He could only guess who sent the package.

As soon as they finished their homework, they sat on the floor. They spread out all of the library books and the material from the package and dug in. By midnight, they had several pages of notes. They had a very busy weekend ahead because they just barely made a dent in the pile of information.

It was early Sunday evening when they gave a sigh of relief. They stood and stretched, trying to get the kinks out of arms and legs from so many hours of sitting.

The more they studied, the more they became intrigued with these far off, remote lands. It was Tibet that seemed to interest them the most. It is a land populated by rugged, fiercely independent people who were invaded by the Red Chinese in 1959 when the people revolted against Chinese rule that began in 1950. It seemed they had simply gotten fed up with their new masters and tried to kick them out of their country, but they were no match for the mighty Chinese army.

The leaders of many countries saw the invasion coming. In 1957, they persuaded the Dalai Lama, Tibet's spiritual leader, to escape to Darjeeling in India.

"The escape in itself," Jeff told Trudy, "would make a great story."

"Wow," Trudy suddenly exclaimed as she read from her notes. "Listen to this. Tibet is almost ten times larger than the state of New York and twice the size of France. It has a population of only three million, and more than half the country is a desolate plateau called the Change Tang. Now, get this. The average elevation of the plateau is more than 15,000 feet. Can you imagine, 15,000 feet? Tibet is surrounded on three sides—the north, west and south—by towering mountain ranges. The tallest are the Himalayas, which are on the southern border. That's where we trekked in Nepal, and Tibet is on the other side. The Change Tang is mostly a rocky, barren wilderness; what growth there is, is just a bunch of stunted bushes, and there isn't much of that. Tibet is often called the roof of the world. Man, I can sure understand why. This place sounds like something from another planet and just about as hard to get to.

"Hey, wait a minute," Trudy exclaimed excitedly, "here's something else. Did you know that almost all of the great rivers in Asia . . . the Yangtze, Yellow, Mekong and even the Brahmaputra, plus a few more, all flow out of Tibet?"

They sat and compared notes. They formed the opinion that Tibet was a huge land of empty wastes and gigantic mountains. It was windy, cold, and desolate. There was still very little is known about the far off, secret place. Although the Tibetan people hated their Chinese conquerors, the ones who hated them the most were the Khambans, who live in eastern Tibet. They were even more fierce and independent than the rest of the Tibetan people.

"Wait a minute," Jeff said excitedly, "the guy I met from Tibet, Dorje, he said he was a Khamban. He even told me the Khambans were really tough and feared. The Chinese were afraid of them because they were the ones who were carrying out the guerrilla raids against them."

Things began to fall into place. Jeff had the feeling that Dorje was someone special, a born leader. He certainly seemed to have an air of confidence about him. He made Jeff feel like he could get a person out of any kind of jam. He didn't talk down to Jeff and make him feel ignorant. He seemed to have that rare quality of being able to make a complete stranger immediately trust and respect him, which was normally not an easy thing to do. Jeff told all of this to Trudy. She nodded her head and said that she knew exactly what he meant.

Early one evening several days later, the phone rang. It was Dorje. He said that he was Professor so-and-so and wanted to meet with Jeff that very night. Jeff, of course, knew he meant at 9 p.m. at the front door of the library.

He decided to jog over, which took about fifteen minutes. On his way, he had the strange feeling he was being followed. He tried to think of other things, but try as he would, he could not get rid of the feeling. He tried to tell himself it was only his imagination. If he had only known just how true the feeling really was.

Jeff almost fell over backward when Dorje asked him point blank if he could be ready to go in three days.

"You bet," Jeff answered, trying unsuccessfully to hide the excitement in his voice.

Dorje reached inside his sweatshirt and pulled out a sealed envelope. "These are your instructions," he said. "Read them carefully; memorize and follow them to the letter. When you have memorized them, burn them. It may sound somewhat dramatic, but we really cannot take any chances."

Without waiting for a reply, Dorje turned and jogged into the darkness.

Jeff just stood where he was for a few minutes, letting it all sink into his head. Finally, he let out a loud, "YES!" He then ran as fast as possible to his front door.

Trudy came over as soon as he called. He was nervous but did not open the envelope until they were both seated on the couch. The typewritten note was short and to the point.

Your plane tickets will be delivered tonight at 11 p.m.

"You will be met when you arrive at your destination. Your contact will ask you if you are Mr. Frank Johnson from Washington, DC. You will answer, 'No. My name is Bruce Clark, and I am from Wisconsin.' You will do exactly as the note, which you will be given tells you to do."

The two of them just sat there looking at each other. After several minutes, Jeff memorized and destroyed the paper as he was instructed.

They both jumped up from the couch when the doorbell rang. It was exactly 11 p.m. No words were spoken as Jeff took the envelope that was handed him and shut the door. Trudy was so anxious; she grabbed the envelope from his hand and tore it open. Inside were two airline tickets. One ticket was to New Delhi, the capital of India. This was surprise enough. The second ticket caused them to stare at each other in stunned silence.

"I can't believe it. I can't believe it," Jeff finally said in a weak voice. Trudy checked out the tickets and told him that they were real. Then she became excited—so excited that she began to jump up and down in the middle of the room, holding the tickets over her head. Her excitement was contagious, and it wasn't long before Jeff joined her.

chapter 5

"Kathmandu, here I come! Kathmandu, here I come," shouted Jeff repeatedly. Suddenly, it dawned on him he had one heck of a lot to do and not much time in which to do it. The first thing Trudy asked him was about his passport: was it still valid, and what about money?

"Yes, I'm sure my passport is still valid," he answered. "Remember, I got it five years ago when I went with my parents to London. I'll go first thing in the morning to get some money out of my savings account."

The jumbo jet made a turn in preparation for its final approach to land. His eyes were glued to the window. The colors of the Indian dusk were a mixture of pastel haze, accented by the many colored lights of the city of New Delhi. It was a breathtaking sight. Jeff could feel the pulse in his temples pounding with excitement. He sensed he was about to begin what would probably be the greatest adventure of his young life.

There was no time for sightseeing. He spent a sleepless night at the airport hotel but rose early enough to make the flight to Nepal.

"Things are going really smooth so far," he thought as he prepared to board the plane. "I was even able to get all of the shots I had to have before I left." He winced as he rubbed his still sore arms.

The twin engines of the Dakota coughed into life as he settled in his seat by the window and buckled his safety belt. The plane was full except for the empty seat beside him. The passenger door was just about to close when a man dressed in a well-cut western suit entered. The pretty Nepalese flight attendant pointed for him to sit in the empty seat. What caught Jeff's eye was the smirk on the man's face when he took his seat. He was Asian, probably Chinese, thought Jeff, and he acted very aloof. Because his attempts at polite conversation were met with a cold stare and total silence, Jeff decided to watch out the window at the passing scene below and ignore the man.

"Just my luck," thought the man in the seat next to Jeff. "I get the only seat left on the plane, and I have to sit next to an American teenager. Well, at least he will not be changing planes with me for the flight to Tibet. I will act as though he did not even exist."

Luckily, the man did not recognize Jeff. He had never seen him up close, and anyway, all American teen-aged males looked the same to Captain Ling.

In the far distance, above the shimmer of heat, Jeff could just make out the lofty, snow-covered peaks of the Himalayas. Finally, the monotonous brown fields they had been flying over gave way to deep green foothills. The pilot gained altitude to get above some turbulence and to have enough height to get over the rising mountain peaks that formed the entrance to Nepal.

Captain Ling heaved a sigh of relief when they climbed above the rough air. He was beginning to feel sick to his stomach, and the last thing he wanted to do was to lose face in front of a Westerner by getting airsick.

It was at that point that Jeff just happened to look at Captain

Ling out of the corner of his eye. He thought to himself that the man's face was taking on a slightly green color.

"Nepal," Jeff sat thinking, "is probably not nearly as wild as Tibet, but it's every bit as formidable in its own way. There are four large rivers and at least fifty-one mountain peaks between 23,000 and 29,000 feet high." Plus, Jeff knew from his recent studies, Nepal also had a hairy area of jungle that was full of snakes and other not-so-nice kinds of creatures. The thought of snakes made him shudder because he really hated snakes.

He was very pleased with himself because he studied all the material on Nepal and Tibet. He remembered the most accessible and populated area in Nepal was called the Central Trough, which was a series of valleys and hills located between the countries lower and inner range of mountains. This, too, was where the richest agricultural and pastureland was found. He almost became smug with himself thinking he had done pretty darn good to study and remember all that stuff.

Lost in his thoughts, Jeff seemed to feel a soothing effect from the drone of the plane's engines. Even so, a feeling of doubt began to creep into his head. What if no one met him when they landed? What if he'd made this trip for nothing? What if they just wanted to get rid of him so he wouldn't try to interfere; get him out of the way so he would not bug them?

He could have gone on and on with the what-ifs, but he began to think at last in a positive way. He knew he would be met. He knew he was going to be able to be a part of the plan to free his parents. He had no knowledge of where, exactly, he would be going once he got to Kathmandu. But wherever the road or trail led, he was willing to go. He knew without a doubt that he was in top physical and mental condition. He knew he had faults and shortcomings, but he had never before felt this new confidence in himself. At the moment, he really felt good about himself and what he was capable of doing.

A slight lurch caused him to look out the window. They were flying between steeply terraced mountains and seemed to be on their landing approach to Kathmandu. The green mountainsides were a pattern of narrow paths with an occasional village of brown thatched buildings. At the low altitude they were flying, the ground looked like a giant multicolored patchwork quilt.

The plane touched the runway with a jolt and taxied toward a line of low buildings. He could see several groups of people waiting. Would his contact be among them?

Kathmandu sits at an elevation of 4,500 feet above sea level. To Jeff's joy, the temperature outside the plane was much more pleasant than the hot, muggy air he left in New Delhi.

The airport terminal was a throng of color. There were red-robed Buddhist Monks, Indians in spotless white, and Nepalese officials and businessmen in tailored jackets and well-fitted riding breeches. To Jeff's eyes, the terminal seemed like a carnival. It was very exciting.

"What should I do?" Jeff questioned himself. "Just take it easy and be casual," he guessed. "I'll probably be contacted here in the terminal. I only hope I don't forget the password."

It was not long before he felt a tug on his shirtsleeve. His heart skipped a beat. It was only a small boy selling trinkets. He began to get the jitters.

"Settle down. Settle down," he kept repeating to himself.

It happened while he was waiting to pick up his baggage.

"Excuse me," a quiet voice said from beside him. "Are you Mr. Frank Johnson from Washington, D.C.?"

Jeff's mind went blank. The slender young man with a well-trimmed black beard just stood looking at Jeff. Finally, after a long pause, he remembered and was able to answer.

"No. My name is Bruce Clark, and I am from Wisconsin."

A faint smile crossed the bearded face as he held out his hand, which Jeff shook. He felt the paper being pressed into his palm.

The young man wished him good luck in a friendly voice and headed for the exit.

"Okay. I can handle this," Jeff muttered repeatedly to himself. He looked for a place so he could read the note without being noticed. It read:

> *Go directly to the Royal Hotel and check in. You will be contacted.*

After checking through customs, he found a taxi. When they pulled in front of the hotel, the driver took enough money from the coins Jeff held out in his hand to cover the cost of the trip from the airport. He handed the driver some extra coins for a tip and judged by the smile on the driver's face that he was being very generous. He walked toward the hotel's entrance. A friendly bellboy met him and carried his luggage inside. The bellboy would not let Jeff help in any way. Checking in did not take long. He was a little unsure but decided to stay in his room and wait to be contacted. Nothing happened the first day. It was not until late the following afternoon that there was a tap on his door. Upon opening the door, Jeff was relieved to see who was standing there.

"Hello, Jeff. I see you made the trip okay. I'm sorry I took so long getting to you, but I have had a lot to do."

"Dorje," Jeff almost yelled. "Man, am I glad to see you. I was really getting worried. What a surprise. You are the last person I expected to see."

In his wild enthusiasm, Jeff almost yanked Dorje's arm off as he pulled him into his room. He felt he had just been found by a long lost friend.

They ended up talking late into the night. Dorje told Jeff that he had indeed been followed that night.

"His name is Captain Ling," Dorje said, "and it looks like he will not be following anyone for a while. He is the person who sat next to you on the flight from New Delhi. He is the right-hand man of Colonel Chin and almost as ruthless and cold-blooded. For some reason, he is on his way back to Tibet. We know that he did not know it was you he was sitting next to on the plane. By the way, you did an excellent job in disguising your departure from America. You were not even followed. I think your friend Trudy was a big help. Anyway," he continued, "to get back to Captain Ling. We don't know exactly why he is on his way back to Tibet, but we think it just might have something to do with your parents. I can't say for sure. Colonel Chin is a strange man with a very warped mind. The only person he really seems to trust or has any kind of confidence in his whole organization is Ling. We strongly believe that it was Ling who masterminded the kidnaping of your mother."

Jeff did not even ask Dorje how he came to know all of what he just told him.

When Dorje did leave, he told Jeff to be ready by 8 a.m. because he was going to take him to the town of Trisuli, which was about a forty-five-minute drive from Kathmandu. Why? He did not say, but Jeff said he would be waiting.

The next morning while he waited, his thoughts turned to the prior evening. Jeff not only told Dorje the story of his life, but Dorje really got more into his past than when he talked about it when they first met. Jeff learned Dorje was smuggled out of Tibet into Nepal to stay with relatives and attend a missionary school. If the Chinese had caught them, they would probably have been shot. When he finished his schooling, he was sent to England to further his education and attend one of that country's major universities, where he got a degree in law.

He mentioned to Dorje that this must have cost his parents a lot of money.

Dorje very humbly replied, "They were very rich, so money was no problem."

Dorje never forgot he was a Tibetan—a Tibetan Khamban. To Jeff, this last remark meant nothing when Dorje first told him, but now it did. He told Dorje he had read about the Khambans in the material he studied before leaving home. The things he read, though, were not very flattering.

Dorje then said the Khambans are a very fearless people who live mostly in Eastern Tibet in the region called Kham. Kham was very remote and one of the wildest parts of Tibet. It was also very beautiful. He said again that if a Khamban likes you, he would go to any lengths to prove his friendship. But, if he does not like you . . . look out. The Khambans certainly hated the Chinese, but they especially despised Colonel Chin.

After getting his degree, Dorje did not practice law because his heart was in Tibet. What he wanted to do was to try to help his people. He spent as much time as he could in his father's valley, teaching English to the people and setting up a school.

There was a knock at the door, but it was only the maid to see if she could begin cleaning the room. He sent her away, telling her to come back in half an hour. He thought he should be gone by then.

Dorje told him where his parents and people live was such a remote, unexplored part of Tibet, the Chinese didn't even know of its existence. A few years ago, Colonel Chin set up his headquarters in a lonely monastery not far from the valley and had forced the lamas to leave. He was very cruel to them and tortured many of those who refused to go.

"What about your valley?" Jeff had asked. "Did this Colonel Chin find out about it?"

"Even though it is a large valley, it is located in such a secret place he has never found nor knows anything about it. I am very certain no outsider will ever find it. That is unless he is taken there by one of us," he added with a grin on his face.

Jeff had wondered how far the monastery was from the valley, and Dorje told him it was a very long day's ride over a very little-known trail.

"A constant watch is kept on the monastery by our people who work there." Then he said, "Very little goes on as far as Colonel Chin is concerned that we do not know about. That is how we found out first about your father and then, of course, your mother. We also know that Chin has set up a laboratory with the most modern equipment available for your parents. We really have a first class spy network to keep an eye on the evil colonel. Something we do not know is whether or not he has forced them yet to continue their experiments."

This last statement caused a sense of helplessness to come over Jeff.

chapter 6

The jeep Dorje drove certainly looked like it had seen better days.

"Is this thing safe?" Jeff asked with a laugh.

"Well, if we break down somewhere on the road, you're in such good shape that you can run and get some help," he kidded.

Dorje wore a fox fur hat that made him look even taller than he was. A wide, gray sash was tied around his waist, and his shirt looked like it consisted of homespun wool. His long, tight pants were stuffed into high, soft leather boots. In his belt were a small Tibetan sword and a mean curved dagger, both in leather cases. He told Jeff that he was dressed as a true Khamban.

"There is a large camp of Tibetan refugees at Trisuli," Dorje told Jeff as he eased the jeep out of the city. "They are friends and have helped me many times in the past. They are expecting us. What we need are several strong men to carry our supplies and who will be able to get us to our destination. It's the first of May, and we have to get a move on. We could still hit bad weather on the high passes, but it can snow any time of the year. Once we get to the other side, the chance of getting snow is very rare."

Once over the first ridge, they began a hairy, cliff-clinging drive down and around steep tree-covered hillsides and green valleys. The multitude of rice paddies and darker green fields of maize reminded Jeff of a giant checkerboard. The fields would begin at the valley's floor and stair-step to the very mountaintops. Small, well-built Nepalese women and children worked the fields side by side. The going was often very slow. When they finally reached Trisuli, Dorje drove straight to the Tibetan camp where a group of men greeted them. Jeff thought these men were the camp's leaders. He got the idea that because of the reverent, respectful way Dorje was treated, he must be someone special.

They were led to a large, round tent that was guarded by a ferocious black dog. Inside, Jeff was introduced to the small group. To his surprise, they all spoke at least some English. After the formalities were out of the way, they were served tea. It was not like any tea he had ever tasted before. Later, they told him rancid yak butter was added to the tea, and that was why it had a very salty and bitter taste. It was the staple drink of Tibet, Dorje had explained. While all the others seemed to enjoy the scalding hot concoction, it was all Jeff could do to keep from vomiting. He knew he had to keep it down or he would surely lose face, and that was the last thing he wanted to do.

When Dorje got down to the business they had come for, all the talking was done in Tibetan. Because he could not understand what they were saying, he kept a close watch on Dorje's face. Only once did he see him frown. The meeting took about an hour. When they were leaving to drive back to Kathmandu, Jeff asked how things had gone.

"Very well," Dorje replied, "very well."

Dorje was silent for several miles, deep in thought. When they reached a wide spot in the road, he pulled over and parked. Looking Jeff straight in the eye, he said, "I have really got to warn you that what lies ahead is not going to be a picnic. It is very dangerous just to reach Tibet. Not only is the trail very treacherous, there are the weather and the possibility of running into a Chinese army patrol. If this should happen, it would be every man for himself. If you are captured, you could possibly be shot as a spy. There are unknown side trails that we may be forced to take. They are little more than wild animal trails and very dangerous. When we try to free your parents . . . well, I don't even want to think what might happen to you if Colonel Chin's men captured you. There certainly may be some of us who do not make it, but that is the chance we will have to take. Now, if you want to stay behind in Kathmandu and wait until I return, I will certainly understand."

"No way," answered Jeff firmly. "I am going with you, and I don't think I'll be any problem. I'll do what you tell me to do and will do my fair share."

"I was hoping you would say that," he said, slapping Jeff on the back. He gunned the engine and headed up the twisting, dusty road.

It was late when Dorje dropped Jeff off at his hotel. When he opened the door to his room, he let out a yell. "Not this again," he said in a loud, angry voice.

The place was a mess. It looked like a whirlwind had been in the room. "Whoever did this could have at least been a little neater," he sighed as he set about picking things from the floor.

The more he had to pick up, the angrier he got. He didn't even think about being scared. Now, more than ever, he knew he was going. No one was going to scare him into changing his plans.

Early the next morning, Jeff opened his door to a loud knock. He was handed a piece of paper by one of the hotel staff. When Jeff asked who had given it to him, all he would say was that the person did not give his name.

Be at the entrance to Swanabunath Temple at 9:30 this morning. I will find you.

That was all the note said. Jeff had heard of the temple and knew of the hundreds of temples in Kathmandu. This particular one, all visiting Buddhists were sure to visit. It was the oldest of all the temples and the most sacred.

The temple looked very imposing where it sat on a solitary hill surrounded by a flat plain. Its gilded roofs reflected sharply in the bright sun.

As the taxi driver approached the impressive temple, he said he would wait for Jeff.

Jeff began to climb a long series of stairs. On each side were strange stone gods and weird-looking mythical beasts. Very spooky, he thought to himself. He was glad there were lots of people around. Finally, he reached the top step. He stopped to try to get his bearings, look things over, and try to decide just what to do next.

He did not have to wonder for long. He jumped when he felt someone grab his arm.

"Come with me," he stated hurriedly. Jeff hesitated for just an instant before following the stranger. He had no idea where he was being lead, but wherever it was, whoever was leading him was in a hurry to get there. Their pace was more like running than walking.

As they rounded a far corner of the building, someone grabbed Jeff from behind. His arms were pinned by someone very powerful. He was told not to struggle and he would not be hurt.

A blindfold was placed across his eyes, and his hands were tied behind his back. He was stumbling along, being led by his captors, when he heard two thuds, a groan, and the sound of two limp bodies hitting the ground.

His hands were quickly untied and the blindfold removed.

Before he could say anything, the burly Tibetan who had just saved him told him firmly in very good English to go back to his hotel; Dorje would see him soon. The man walked off with Jeff still slightly dazed. He did not even have a chance to thank him.

Not long after he returned to his room, Dorje arrived. "The people responsible for this little episode," he told Jeff, "are well known to us. They have no connection at all with Colonel Chin. What this group of hoodlums does is kidnap foreigners and hold them for ransom. They must have had a lookout at the airport who spotted you as an American. So, since all Americans are supposed to be wealthy, they just waited to carry out their scheme. I do not think they will bother you again," he said with a wink, adding they were the ones who also broke into his room.

Dorje told Jeff that for his own protection, one of his people was following him, just in case. Jeff was certainly glad someone was around when he needed them, and he told Dorje so.

While they sat talking, out of nowhere, Dorje said they would be leaving in two days. This really took Jeff by surprise, and he felt excited. Dorje then handed Jeff the large package he had with him and told Jeff to open it.

"What's all of this stuff?" he asked of the strange looking clothing he took from the package.

"That," replied Dorje, "is what you will wear on the long trip to my valley. Those are the same kind of clothes a Tibetan Khamban would wear. You must look as much like a Tibetan as possible. I only hope we do not run into any Chinese patrols. If we do, they may very well spot you, and that would not be good. No, that would not be good at all. What you have to do is to try to blend in with the rest of the party as much as possible. We do not want anyone to become suspicious. There are spies all over. Even the most remote village might have its spy."

After Dorje left, Jeff tried on his new outfit. He found the wool-lined, yak-skin pants very comfortable. The parachute-silk shirt, which is the mark of a modern Khamban warrior, fit quite nicely. So did the knee-length boots and long sheepskin coat. Looking in the mirror, he thought he looked quite wild, especially when he put on the tall, fox-fur cap with the large earflaps. The clothing was just what one needed in the often harsh climate of Tibet.

Dorje told him not to bring anything with him that might cause anyone to become suspicious. So Jeff told Dorje he would leave what he should not bring. Jeff did, however, buy a few things he thought might come in handy.

He asked about buying food for the trip, but Dorje told him that had all been taken care of. Jeff wondered why Dorje had a weird smile on his face when he told him this. He guessed he would find out soon enough.

On the day they were leaving, it was still well before sunrise when they finished loading the jeep with Jeff's equipment. He was told all of the other supplies were already at the Tibetan camp and were packed and ready to go.

During the drive, Dorje told Jeff they could not leave until they got word all was clear.

"What does that mean?" Jeff asked.

"It means," answered Dorje, "we have to make sure there are no Chinese patrols on the trail we will be taking once we arrive in Tibet. It would be very risky and certainly not very wise to go without knowing. Still, you never know for sure. A patrol might show up at any time or anywhere. We always have to be careful."

"How will you know when it is okay to leave?"

"A runner will let us know. We have a very good human telegraph system set up in Tibet, as well as a reliable spy network, which, of course, is unknown to the Chinese."

When they arrived, the camp was a beehive of activity. A Tibetan whom Dorje introduced as Sedar, head of the porters, came running to the jeep. Jeff noticed the three of them were dressed almost identically.

"We have received word," he said excitedly. "The trail is all clear. But we must leave immediately because a patrol of Chinese soldiers is to leave within a week to check out the upper pass. I have everything ready to go, and the men are just waiting for their instructions.

"Good work," Dorje complimented. "We will leave in one hour. Tell the men."

chapter 7

The weather when they left was clear and warm, but on the higher passes it could change very quickly. The trail out of camp was quite steep and became steeper the higher they climbed. Jeff knew this first part of the trail would be a real test for him. After a few hours of steady climbing, they could look down on the Tibetan camp. The tents looked like small, dark dots. The four porters carrying their equipment moved at a steady, ground-eating pace. It was nearly dark when they came to a flat area just off the trail. That was where they would spend their first night.

Jeff was hungry and thirsty. He had not a thing to eat since early morning, and what water he had he drank was from a few small streams they crossed.

The evening meal was not a total surprise. He had read about what the main Tibetan diet consisted of, and he felt it was something he would have to deal with when the time came. Now was the time. He had to either eat what was given him or go hungry.

It was Dorje who came to his aid as they sat around the campfire with the others for that first meal. It was served blistering hot and smelled awful. Dorje told him it was tea with rancid yak butter added, just like he had the day at the Tibetan camp. Next, he was handed a good-sized ball of gooey dough made from barley.

"This is called tsampa, and do what I do," Dorje told him. He took some of the dough, rolled it into a bite-sized ball, dipped it into his tea, and popped it into his mouth.

Jeff had learned as a kid that whenever he ate anything he did not like, holding his breath until he swallowed it seemed to help. He thought about doing this but realized he would be holding his breath an awful lot. So into his mouth he gingerly placed the small ball after soaking it in his tea. To his relief, it was not too bad at all. To drink the scalding tea was another matter, though. Dorje told him the tea and the tsampa would keep up his strength.

"Get used to them because we will have tsampa at almost every meal, and we will be drinking several cups of tea a day."

Just like at the Tibetan camp, it was all he could do to keep that first cup down. But he had to admit after finishing his tea and tsampa, he felt much stronger. It also seemed to give him that something extra to ward off the cold wind that had suddenly sprang up. His whole insides felt warm. Like Dorje and the others, he actually had several more cups of the scalding brew and even began to like its bitter, salty taste.

Because he was supposed to blend in and be taken for a Tibetan, Jeff had not brought his sleeping bag. Instead, he slept like the others in their roomy robes close to the fire on the bare ground.

Actually, he slept quite well and was up with the others before dawn. Breakfast was the same as the evening meal. After they had all had a third cup of tea, they were ready to hit the trail.

At first, the Tibetans seemed to be shy toward him. When they saw that Jeff was being just like one of them and doing his share, they started to lose their shyness and began to be friendly. All of them spoke at least some English, so he was able to talk to them. He liked them. Already, he was beginning to feel like he fit in and was really trying to do his share.

The narrow, rocky trail led upward toward the high peaks of the Himalayas. Jeff asked Dorje how many days it would take before they crossed into Tibet.

"By the route we will be taking, and if all goes well, it would take four long days of hard walking."

Jeff wondered just what he meant by "if all went well."

They had only been on the trail for a few hours when they met two Tibetans coming from the opposite direction. After giving the traditional Tibetan greeting of sticking one's tongue out, they called a halt while Dorje held a quick conference with them. At the end of their talk, by the look on Dorje's face, it appeared the information they had given him might be very serious.

After the two Tibetans left, Dorje called Jeff and the others together. It seemed that there was a newly manned police outpost only a few miles up the trail. They were checking out everyone before they let them pass. This was not good news. They would have to make a detour.

"There is a little known and used trail," Dorje said. "It is dangerous, but it seems to be the only way." He asked if they were all willing, and they were.

Jeff had no idea what to expect. So far, he had been able to keep up with the hardy Tibetans. When they reached the new trail, or what was supposed to be a trail, he really had his doubts.

The narrow, thread-thin path seemed to lead forever higher. They struggled, and at times half crawled, for three days. At night, they slept wherever they could find a place. Never was it level. It was in the late afternoon of the fourth day when they finally reached the summit. There was not a tree, shrub, or living thing to be seen. It was where they would have to camp for the night. Thankfully, there was a small cave close by where they could seek shelter.

As they sat huddled around their meager campfire drinking tea, Jeff sensed that the Tibetans were nervous about something. After several cups, he asked Dorje what the problem might be.

"It is the weather," he answered seriously. "It does not look good at all. The wind is really picking up, the temperature is dropping, and the clouds are building. It looks like we may be in for a snowstorm. We had all better try to get some sleep."

Jeff shivered again as another blast of icy wind enveloped the cave. He had recapped the adventure in his mind from the very beginning to the present. He could only guess what the future might hold. These were his last thoughts as he drifted off to sleep.

Suddenly a hand was on his shoulder, which startled him awake. It was Dorje. "The snow from the storm is very deep, and I think we will all have to take turns breaking a trail," he whispered. "This is nothing new for us, but I thought it best to let you know. I know we will make it, but it will not be easy. I'm going to wake the others. We won't have anything to eat until we get below the snow line. There is just enough fuel left for a small fire, so we will have some hot tea to help warm us and give us strength. Believe me, we will need all of the strength we can get."

They held a council while they drank their tea. The wind and snow had not let up, and Jeff was really thankful for the tea because it did help. It was decided that each one of them would take his turn at trail breaking. Dorje volunteered to go first.

Dorje stood leaning slightly into the wind, holding one of the six-foot wooden staffs they all carried. The wind increased. The stinging effect of the falling snow on their faces felt like a thousand needles. Dorje very carefully forced his way forward through the soft, waist-deep snow a few steps and then plunged the pole down until he found solid ground. He broke forward a few more steps and repeated the maneuver. It was a slow, tiring process. The others followed as close as they dared in single file, tramping the snow to make a trail. Finally, Dorje let the man behind him take his place while he went to the end of the line. Several times, when no bottom could be found with the pole, they would all have to backtrack and begin again. More than once, the one breaking trail would all but disappear into the soft snow and would have to be pulled free by the others. But only a few could do the freeing because of the narrowness of the trail. The Tibetan in front of Jeff was rather frail looking and was probably well into his 60s. When it was his turn to break trail, Jeff was surprised at just how much stamina he had. He really did not think he would last long, but he was able to accomplishing even more than those who had gone before him.

The going got harder—much harder. Before, they had been on narrow yet fairly level ground. Now they were on the side of a steep drop-off. It was a spot that because of the narrowness of the trail would have been dangerous under ideal circumstances. However, with the conditions as they were, it seemed almost suicidal. For once, though, there was a short break in the storm. Jeff looked over the side of the drop-off and was just able to make out the thin line of a river at the very bottom. He knew that if any of them lost their footing, it would be a one-way trip because it was a long, long way down.

"Feel for a hard bottom with the staff, one step at a time," Dorje instructed when it was Jeff's turn to break trail. "Do not hurry. Take your time. If you are not sure, poke around until you are. Remember," he added, "we are on the side of a very steep mountain. Keep probing directly in front of you or just slightly to your left. If you poke too far to the right, you may lose your balance and fall. When you get tired, quit and go to the end of the line. Do not push yourself. It is when you are tired that you are most likely to make a mistake."

It was with mixed feelings that Jeff took the staff. The one thing he knew for sure was he was going to do the best he could. It gave him a good feeling to know all the others were pulling for him.

It was much harder than he thought it would be, and in spite of the cold, he was soon drenched in sweat. He had a very close call and almost went over the side when the pole did not strike anything solid and threw him off balance. Luckily, the Tibetan just behind him was able to grab his arm so he could recover. Otherwise, he would almost certainly have taken that one-way trip to the bottom of the mountain. After that, he was much more careful. Looking back over his shoulder, he could see they had really made progress and the weather was improving. The wind was not blowing as hard, and it had nearly stopped snowing. Things were definitely looking up.

As Dorje had told him, Jeff handed the staff to the next one in line before he became so exhausted that he might make another mistake. The morning was almost gone when the Tibetan breaking the trail let out an excited yell. He was just around a sharp bend and so was hidden from view from the rest of them. Soon, word came back through the line that the snow line was in sight. Jeff not only felt his own excitement but that of the others, also. They all felt a great sense of accomplishment and relief when Dorje called a halt for lunch, their first food of the day. The sun was shining, the snow lay only in patches, and it was actually warm. The memory of the cold and danger they just conquered was almost forgotten, but not quite. They knew there were foes other than nature that might soon have to be faced.

In celebration of their recent feat, they had dried strips of yak meat to go along with their tsampa and tea. Jeff ate just as much as the others and even seemed to enjoy it as much as his Tibetan friends. Everyone was talking and laughing because the pressure was off, at least for the time being.

While they were eating, Jeff sat next to Dorje. "Can you tell me just where we are going?" Jeff questioned Dorje with a serious look on his face.

"Yes," Dorje replied after a short pause. "We are going to a very remote, hidden valley in the Khamban area of my country. Like I told you before, it is so remote and hidden that the Chinese have not found out that it even exists. It is very beautiful. We will be staying in the only village in the valley, which is where my parents live. This is where the plans to free your parents will be made."

"Exactly where are my parents?"

"The monastery where they are being held is, as I have said, Colonel Chin's headquarters. It is only about a long, hard day's journey by horseback from my valley. It, too, is in a very remote setting. But we have friends who actually work in the monastery. They keep my father well informed. Oh, by the way," Dorje asked teasingly, "have you ever ridden a horse?"

"Actually, Jeff could ride," he said. Now more than ever he was glad he learned to ride. It was Trudy who got him interested. She took him out to some friends of her parents' farm, which was not too far from town. They had a few excellent horses, and that is where he learned. When the weather was good, he and Trudy often rode several times a week. The owners were glad because it was good exercise for the horses. His answer seemed to please Dorje, and nothing more was said about whether he could ride a horse or not. After lunch, they set off down the snow-less but still very narrow and dangerous trail. Even though they were below the snow line, an icy wind had picked up and was blowing directly into their faces. It was late afternoon and time to camp for the night before it finally died down.

They were in a grove of large pine trees, and it was pleasant and warm sitting around the campfire. The sound of the small stream where they got water, with its swift, cold current running over a bed of rocks, was like music to his ears. He had always loved the sound made by a running stream. Jeff knew he would sleep well that night.

They rose before dawn, feeling well rested and ready for the trail. But first, it was breakfast and, as usual, it was yak butter tea and tsampa. Jeff had to admit to himself that he was actually beginning to enjoy them. In fact, he was getting darned good at making his tsampa into a mouth-sized ball with one hand, wetting it in his tea, and then popping the ball into his mouth. Of this he was very proud, and felt he was almost as good at it as the Tibetans who taught him.

"Eat hearty," Dorje encouraged, "because it is going to be a long, hard day, and we'll not be stopping for lunch."

Time was very important, especially now. They were on the other side of the mountains, and he wanted them to make up as much time as possible. They still had another pass to cross, but because they were on the other side of the Himalayas, the chance of getting another snowstorm was slight. It could get very cold, but it was much drier there. Still, anything could happen, especially in the Himalayas.

Jeff did not think he had ever been so hungry in his life, or for that matter, so hot. It seemed like an eternity ago when they had been struggling so desperately through the snow. Now, even though they were still very high in the mountains, they were out of the snow and it was hot. He found out the sun at this altitude could really be tough.

Dorje told Jeff that the reason for the especially long day was so they could reach a small Tibetan village before dark. "Yes," he said to a surprised Jeff, "we are finally in Tibet."

chapter 8

The trail did not widen and in places was almost nonexistent. They were now high on the side of a canyon and, looking down, Jeff could see a stream or river winding its way through the canyon floor.

The trail began to widen just a bit and seemed to be heading down toward a kind of flat area just above the river. In one day they had gone from deep snow and chilling cold to an area where the trail wound through green, forested mountainsides and really warm weather. The canyon side, on which the trail now hung, was barren of any kind of growth. There was nothing but bare rock walls and the hot, blue sky above. It was getting even hotter. The sun's rays, combined with the bare granite walls of the canyon, created a kind of huge, open-air oven.

To Jeff, walking down the steep side of the trail was just about as hard, if not harder, than walking up the trail. He was glad when it finally began to level out. Jeff was in the lead when he rounded a sharp corner in the trail and almost ran into an elderly Tibetan woman. He let out a surprised yelp and stopped so quickly, Dorje, who was close behind, nearly knocked him down. It was very comical, and they all had a good laugh. Dorje knew the woman and seemed very glad to see her. She seemed just as happy to see him.

They stood off to the side of the trail and talked for several minutes. Jeff watched as the smile on Dorje's face turned to a look of grave concern. When they finished talking, Dorje patted the woman on her shoulder, and she turned and walked down the trail.

Dorje called the group together. He explained to Jeff what he and the woman had been talking about.

"It seems," he began with a very serious tone to his voice, "a Chinese patrol came through her village early this morning. The village is not far around the next bend and sits right on the main trail. The Chinese thankfully do not know about this trail. From now on, we have got to be very careful. The Chinese have many spies. So now more than ever, you have got to act the part of a Tibetan. Try not to speak to anyone, but don't raise any kind of suspicion, either. Just try to blend in."

It was only a short walk to the village. As they entered, all Jeff saw were a few stone shacks located along the edge of the river. This was where they were going to spend the night. They were shown to a small one-room building by one of the villagers. This was where they were to sleep. There was only one problem . . . the hut did not have a roof. If it rained, they would certainly get drenched.

"What a desolate place to live," Jeff thought to himself. He had never seen such a barren spot. Hardly a blade of grass grew, and all he could see were rocks and dirt. He wondered how the few people of the village existed, so he asked Dorje.

"They are smugglers," he answered with a grin on his face, but with a serious tone to his voice. "They bring in hard to get items from India and Nepal. The Chinese patrol that went through here this morning probably bought most of the stuff they had. The Chinese soldiers are the villagers' best customers. They have an arrangement with the Chinese commander for the illegal trade. These villagers, even though they do not look like it, are very wealthy compared to most of the people in Tibet."

That night, the wind howled down the narrow canyon. The fire of dried yak dung was barely large enough to make tea. It certainly did not give off much heat. The stone walls of the roofless hut were meant more for keeping animals in, not for keeping the wind out. Even though it was a cold night, it was still nothing compared to the night they had spent in the cave.

It was long before daylight when Jeff felt a tug at his shoulder. "Help me get the others up," Dorje whispered, "but be very quiet. We have to leave now."

Jeff did not ask any questions but did as he was told. Soon they were on the move. The only sound was the barking of one of the village's mongrel dogs as they walked silently down the trail in the almost total blackness that comes just before dawn. After a few miles of fast walking, they turned off the main path into a narrow side canyon. The going was very rough, but they kept their pace. More than ever, Jeff was thankful that he had worked so hard to get himself into shape. He felt sure of himself, and he now knew he could keep up with the Tibetans.

It was late in the morning, and they were high above the village. Dorje called a halt on the edge of a cliff where they had a good view of the river below and the main trail.

"I thought so," he said with a disgusted tone to his voice. "Look down there," he told Jeff and the others. "See that line of moving dots on the main trail? That's a patrol of Chinese soldiers, and I think they are looking for us."

"How did you know they would be coming?" Jeff questioned.

"Instinct, I guess. But we were betrayed. There certainly must be a Chinese spy living in the village. Thanks to the barking of the village dogs, I heard whomever it was leave not long after we turned in for the night. Undoubtedly, they went looking for the patrol that had recently passed through the village. I don't know if the spy spotted you or not, but we have got to be extra careful from now on. I'm certainly glad to know about this side trail. Now that I know neither the spy nor the Chinese know about it, it makes me feel much better. I wonder if the spy will get into any trouble because we were able to get away in time. If he does, it serves him right."

The straggled line of men labored under the cloudless, deep blue sky. Although Dorje told Jeff they were at an altitude of over 16,000 feet, it was hot. It was the kind of hot that makes you feel like you are shriveling into nothing but loose flesh and bones. There was no shade, only bare rock walls. Their pace slowed to not much more than a crawl, but no one complained. They just kept placing one foot in front of the other. It was like being in a dreamlike trance. No one spoke because it would take too much energy. Jeff thought to himself if he had his choice, though, he would certainly choose being hot rather than cold like the night they spent in the cave.

A halt was called for lunch beside a waterfall. After eating, Jeff and even the Tibetans stripped and took a shower. The shock of the icy water caused his teeth to chatter. Dorje allowed them a little extra time to soak in the large pool beneath the fall. Once they were fully refreshed, Dorje told them their next stop would be in a village where they would not have to worry about spies. They would take a day to rest and repair anything that might need it. Jeff knew he had to do some mending on his shirt because he accidentally caught it on a sharp tree limb. He knew he could use the rest and felt the others would be just as glad to have a day off. Dorje told Jeff that after their day's rest, they would force-march for two days to the village, where they would pick up horses for the two of them to ride the rest of the way. The others would stay in the village until both he and Jeff returned or were sent word to go back without them.

"Horses," Jeff half yelled, "you mean we get to ride horses the rest of the way to your village?"

"You bet," Dorje answered with a laugh. "We ride the last part of the trip in style."

"So," thought Jeff to himself with some sense of pride and relief, "the first part of the adventure is just about at an end. I wonder what the next part will have in store for me."

chapter 9

Instead of improving, the trail often vanished into thin air and had to be searched for. Finally they arrived at the village. They were all exhausted but very thankful to have made it. Now it was fix-it time. They repaired boots and clothing. They gave gifts to the village elders. When they first got to the village, they were told a Chinese patrol had passed through earlier that morning. It was thought it was probably the same one they had spotted earlier, and Dorje told Jeff again he was thankful for knowing about the rarely used trails. Although they were more dangerous and difficult, he said he would rather risk traveling on one of them than running into a Chinese army patrol.

The headman of the village seemed to be a close friend of Dorje's, and they spent much time together. When they were alone, Dorje told Jeff the headman was one of those who had helped him escape to Nepal. He always tried to bring him a special present of some kind. This time, it was a pair of sunglasses. The old man seemed so pleased and proud that Jeff said he was probably going to wear them even when he went to bed.

The next two days were really tough. They were up and on the trail well before sunup. Their first meal was a lunch of dried yak meat eaten on the go. They did not stop for the night until it was almost too dark to see the faint trail. The pace set by the Tibetans was grueling. Jeff had never worked so hard in his life. More than once, he almost called it quits, but somehow he kept placing one foot in front of the other. At times he felt as though he was moving outside his body. When a halt was finally called at the end of that second long day's march, Jeff staggered the last several yards and almost fell flat on his face. He did not even feel like eating because he was so exhausted. When the tsampa and tea were ready, his Tibetan friends insisted he at least try to eat. With some effort he was able to eat his share and drink several cups of tea after which he almost felt like his old self.

That night he slept like he had never slept before. He did not even dream. Like the others, he was up at first light and ready to go. Still, he was very surprised to see that they had camped near the edge of a village. He had been so tired the night before that he did not notice.

While the last village where they camped looked shabby and crude, this one looked tidy and very clean. The houses were of stone and well made. The scenery had changed from bare granite to large groves of scented pine trees and much grass for the herds of yak, which the people raised. Yaks, Jeff discovered, looked like large, unkempt cattle with long, dark hair. He was told they could only live at very high altitudes. The people use the yaks' fur to spin into yarn to make clothing. The milk was used for making butter, which, when rancid, was put into their tea. The bulky beast was also used as a pack animal, and because wood was often very scarce, dried yak dung was used for making fires. The yak was a very useful and prized animal. The people of this village, along with their yaks, had large herds of sheep.

Jeff took a short walk and was surprised to see just how much the scenery had changed. It reminded him of the states of Montana and Idaho, where he had vacationed with his parents. The people here seemed much better off than most of the people they had come in contact with. They were much better dressed and very friendly.

Jeff was curious, so he asked Dorje why these people seemed so much different from others they had met.

"Well, these people are Khambans," he began with an almost humble tone to his voice. "We Khambans, as I told you, have always been feared by other Tibetans. Khambans are usually happy and are good people who are much like the legendary Robin Hood and his men. Khambans are known to steal, but more often than not, they steal from the rich and treat the average and the poor Tibetans with respect. Much of what they steal, just like in the stories written about Robin Hood, is given to the poor and needy."

That night, Dorje attended a short meeting with the village elders. After the meeting was over, Dorje took Jeff aside and told him the trail ahead seemed to be all clear of patrols, at least until they reach the trail that led to Tibet's capital, Lhasa. They would be on that trail for only a short distance before they cut off onto the hidden trail that led to his village. They would have to be very careful not to leave any trace of cutting off the main trail. They would be on horseback and, of course, horses hooves are easily seen.

"Luckily, most of the main trail is carpeted with pine needles, so we will not have to worry. It is only the last hundred yards or so that we have to be concerned."

"Where are the horses?" questioned Jeff, trying to act calm and keep the excitement from his voice.

"Above the village at the end of a short, narrow canyon is a meadow. This is where the horses are kept so the Chinese won't find and take them."

"What about the main trail? What if we should happen to meet a Chinese patrol? How will we hide?"

"We only have to travel a few hours on the main trail," Dorje replied reassuringly. "As I have said, for now, anyway, the trail looks all clear. If by some chance we should meet a patrol, we will act just as though we belong right where we are, but you play dumb. I will do all the talking. It may not sound like a very good plan, but we just have to take the chance." Dorje added that once they were on the trail that led to his village, they would only have one thing to be concerned with, and that was just getting there.

"You told me before that your village is in a very remote place. How remote do you mean?"

"From right here, where we are standing," Dorje answered, "it will take us at least two and possibly three days, depending on the weather, to reach the valley where my village is located. The trail is known only to a very few, trusted outsiders. Like the trails we have been forced to use, it is not on any map. It has never been explored by any outsiders. Besides, unless you lived there, were taken there by a Khamban, or were invited to visit for some reason, it would be extremely unlikely anyone would find it. It is just too remote. Anyway, you will see for yourself once we get there."

"Wow," exclaimed Jeff, "it sounds remote, all right." Again he asked, "Just where is the place my parents are being held?"

Dorje then led Jeff to a flat area of dirt. He took a stick, drew a map, and patiently began to explain. "Here is the trail to Lhasa. Here is where we are, and here is where the trail to my valley connects with the trail to Lhasa. Like I told you, once we reach the trail it will take us at least two and possibly three days to reach the valley. Now," he continued, "as you come into the valley, on the left is a high ridge of mountains. On the other side of this ridge of mountains is a small valley. This is where the monastery is located that serves as Colonel Chin's headquarters and where your parents are being kept prisoners. That, too, as I said, is a very secret place. Since the Chinese army invaded Tibet, they have destroyed most of the monasteries. Had they found this one, they would surely have destroyed it, as well. And Colonel Chin is certainly not going to tell where it is because he uses it as his secret headquarters. I don't know how Colonel Chin found it, but when he did, he forced the monks to leave. He told them if they did not leave, he would kill them all and destroy the monastery. So what else could they do? It takes one long day to get from my village to the monastery, providing the weather on the high pass is good."

Dorje continued to tell Jeff that once they were on the trail to his valley, they would still have some pretty rough going, but it would be nothing compared with what they had already been through.

"Why are we going to ride horses if it's going to be so rough?"

"Because," began Dorje with a grin on his face, "the horses we will be riding are horses from my valley. They have the stamina and are as sure-footed as the much smaller Tibetan ponies. However, our horses are much bigger and stronger. As you may have noticed, we Khambans are quite a bit bigger than the average Tibetan. So we ride horses that are much larger than the average Tibetan horse. Anyway, to answer your original question, the horses we will be riding belong to me. Please believe me. I am not bragging, but they are probably among the best horses in all of Tibet. And Jeff," he added, "I hope you can ride well, because when we free your parents, we will have to make a run for it. Colonel Chin's men have a few horses, but they are not nearly as good as ours. Colonel Chin also has a helicopter he uses to come and go from the monastery. If it happens to be there when we free your parents, we will somehow have to put it out of commission. We can outrun their horses, but certainly not a helicopter."

Dorje let out a sigh of relief when Jeff told him both his parents grew up on ranches and were excellent riders.

Along with their normal evening meal of tsampa and yak-butter tea, they had meat. It was roasted lamb—real meat. It was the best meat Jeff had ever eaten. He ate so much he felt like he was going to burst, but he did not care. He enjoyed every single bite. That night he slept like a log.

Early the next morning, he awoke to the sound of horses' hooves. After a quick breakfast, they mounted their horses. Jeff was given a large, muscular, bay-colored mount, while Dorje's horse was an equally striking chestnut.

"These," Jeff said to himself, "are two of the finest horses I've ever seen."

He knew without asking that these were horses that could be trusted and relied upon under any kind of circumstance. The packhorse was much smaller and looked rather shaggy compared to their own mounts.

Dorje noticed how Jeff looked at the smaller horse. He told him not to worry. It was a Tibetan pony and just as able to handle itself as the ones they were riding.

Dorje led the way with the packhorse in the middle. Jeff wondered if Dorje was as excited as he was about being on horseback. He was about to ask but thought better of it.

Before they mounted, Dorje told Jeff never to whip the horse and not to use the reins unless he had to. Instead, he should talk to the horse in a soothing tone, using the few Tibetan words taught him. Indicating the direction he wanted the horse to go was done by touching that side of his neck. It was not long before Jeff and the horse began to get used to each other. It only took a short while for him to realize he had never had the privilege of riding such a fine animal.

They rode through a valley green with lush grass and dotted by stands of tall pine trees. The air was cool and refreshing. It was good to be on the move, and the going was easy. After a few uneventful hours, they turned into a narrow canyon with a stream of clear, ice-cold water running down its center. They stopped there. Dorje told Jeff to wait while he went back to erase any sign of their having entered the canyon. He returned shortly and said that he got rid of the hoof prints.

"Is this the trail to your village?" Jeff questioned.

"Yes," he replied. "This is the first part of the trail, but it's really not what you would call a trail. What we do is follow this canyon to its head, cross a wide-open space, and then enter the part that leads into the valley. There is another way in and out of the valley, but it is seldom used. It is really only to be used in an emergency.

Actually, the going was not really that bad. There were a few places where they had to dismount and lead the horses. When they and the animals grew too hot, they would stop and douse themselves with cold water and give the horses a rest. After several hours, they stopped for a light meal. It was then it dawned on Jeff that he did not know the name of this horse.

"Your horse is named Homey, which means 'flowery horse.' The name of my horse is Flash. As you have probably gathered by now, both Homey and Flash are very special horses."

"You can say that again," replied Jeff. "I have never ridden a horse that seemed to possess so much horse-sense." They both had a good laugh at this last statement.

The trail began to get rougher and steeper. The canyon walls seemed to be closing in on them. Dorje finally called a halt and said that they would have to lead the horses until the canyon leveled out. The stream's flow was more restricted, and the trail often led up the middle. Sweat was pouring off Jeff's forehead. Just as he was about to ask for a rest stop, Dorje said it was getting late. He said that around the next bend was a nice, flat area where they would camp for the night. Those words gave Jeff the strength he needed. When they reached the level spot, he noticed that even Dorje was breathing a little hard, but their horses looked just as fresh as when they first began that morning.

The flat area where they were to spend the night was located several feet above the bottom of the canyon. It was a good thing it was because it rained during the night. The level of the stream rose, so they could not continue until early the next afternoon when the water level had dropped.

"This means we will have to spend another night in the canyon," Dorje said as they sat around a fire and talked. They were trying to kill time until the water dropped. "But," he continued, "the worst part is behind us. From now on, the going is easy. We get to ride all the way except for one short stretch where we will camp for the night."

It was very late the following afternoon when they led their horses out of the mouth of the canyon onto the beginning of a mile wide, grassy plane. Clumps of pine forest were separated by open areas of green grass that reached all the way to the belly of the horses. They could see several small herds of wild yaks lazily wandering about.

"This is where we will camp for the night," Dorje declared. "We will start early in the morning and should reach my valley around noon. Once we cross this plain, it's all down hill, and most of it is very easy."

The sense of excitement Jeff heard in Dorje's voice caused a tremble of the same to pass through his body. They were almost there. He could hardly believe it.

That night around their small campfire, Dorje told Jeff about what it was like growing up a Khamban in one of the most remote parts of Tibet.

"It was a wonderful way to grow up," he stated. "From the time when I was five-years-old, I always had a horse. Perhaps I was more fortunate than many boys my age, but you see, my parents are what you would call 'of royal blood.' My father ruled a large area of Khamba. He is very much loved and respected by all who know him. I guess I had what you might call a perfect childhood. What more could I ask for? I had the mountains, my home, and freedom. Most Tibetans lost their freedom when the Chinese invaded. Like I told you before, when I was fourteen years old, my parents sent me to Nepal to go to school. My parents, of course, still lived in the valley, and it's been a while since I have been back. I am really looking forward to seeing them; but then, it will be good to see everyone."

"Will you ever move back to your valley to live?" Jeff questioned.

"Perhaps, when my work is complete. I would like nothing better than to stay. I like the outside world, but I could never live in it for the rest of my life. I guess I'm a true Khamban. Even though I have spent much of my life away from the valley, it is my home and always will be. When I really think about it, there is no place I would rather be. I love the mountains, I love my people and I love Tibet. But . . . it's men like Colonel Chin, men who care nothing about anyone or anything but themselves and their evil gains that make me fear for the future."

Even though they were both tired, it was so relaxing sitting by the fire and talking that neither wanted to go to sleep. Finally, they decided they had better because they had to be up with the sun.

Thoughts raced through Jeff's head as he lay trying to fall asleep. Looking up at the sky, the stars were so bright they looked like a huge sheet of silver foil. His last thought before finally drifting off into a deep slumber was of his parents. He hoped they were alive and well.

Daylight was just creeping over the mountains when Jeff awoke to the sound of the stomping of their horses' hooves. They were, it seemed, anxious to get on the trail. Dorje awoke at the same time and for the same reason. After a hurried breakfast, they saddled and bridled the horses, loaded the packhorse, and were on their way.

There were wild flowers everywhere in all colors and sizes. In the far distance, they could see a range of snow and ice-clad peaks. Jeff asked if they had to ride very far before they reached the valley.

"No," came the reply, "we don't have to go very far at all. Actually, the valley is just through a narrow gorge," he added, pointing his finger as they came to the top of a low rise. "The mouth of the gorge is very hard to find. You have to be right on top of it before you realize where it is."

It was a pleasant and easy ride. The horses were feeling frisky, so they let them have their head. Jeff had never ridden a horse with such speed. The wind whistled in his ears as they ran neck and neck smoothly across the plane. More than once they caused a herd of wild yaks to lumber clumsily out of their way. He was amazed at how well the packhorse kept up with them.

Jeff did not even see the entrance to the gorge until they were right on top of it. Dorje dismounted and told Jeff to lead the horses into the dark passage. He said he would take some tree branches and erase any trace of hoof prints just as a precaution. There was not much room to spare when Dorje squeezed past Jeff and the horses. He would walk at the head while Jeff took up the rear. After a mile of slow zigzagging, the walls began to widen, and suddenly they were out in bright sunlight. They both stood blinking their eyes and tried to adjust to the brightness.

The scene that unfolded caused a gasp of disbelief to escape from Jeff's throat.

chapter 10

"Welcome to my valley," Dorje said with a tone of humble pride in his voice. "We only have a few miles to go now before we reach my village, but let's just sit here for a few minutes so you can take a good look."

They were a few hundred feet above the valley's floor. The view was absolutely spectacular. He had never seen anything so awesome.

"I visited Yosemite Park one summer with my parents," he said in a hushed whisper, "but even Yosemite does not compare with this. I just do not understand how a place could be so beautiful."

In the panorama below them, patches of forest were interlaced with sparkling clear streams that wound through the greenest grass, which was heavily carpeted with multicolored wild flowers. There was the sound of all kinds of birds singing. Herds of horses were mixed in with several herds of grazing yaks and sheep. Dorje pointed to several fruit orchards and in the far distance, the golden gleam of ripe fields of barley. All of this was surrounded by high, jagged, snow-capped mountains. To Jeff, the valley looked everything like a paradise on earth should look.

"I thought," began Jeff, "that Tibet was nothing but a high, rugged, almost barren plain. At least that's the picture I got from reading all of the stuff I read."

"Most of Tibet," Dorje replied, "is like that, but there are some areas in the mountains that are like what you see below. However, this valley is certainly the exception and not the rule."

While they sat taking in the view, Dorje told Jeff the valley was always lush and green and hardly ever got any snow.

"The winters are very mild," he said, "not cold like so much of Tibet. And unlike much of Tibet, we get plenty of rain. This valley seems to have its own weather pattern. I miss it when I'm away, and it seems like I'm away most of the time now. It's time we start for the village, but I have to give the signal first. Even though you cannot see them, the entrance to the valley is always guarded."

Dorje gave the signal by raising both his arms three times. "Now," he said, "we can go."

The ride was as pleasant as you could ask for. The air was cooled by a gentle breeze, which was filled with the scent of flowers and the sound of birds. It was all very, very peaceful. So peaceful that Jeff became so content that he almost forgot why he was there. They crossed several clear streams and rode by several small lakes and ponds whose surfaces were clustered by flocks of wild ducks. Bees were busy flying from flower to flower, and brightly colored butterflies were fluttering everywhere. The place seemed a haven for wildlife.

After some time, they entered a deeply wooded area. When they rode out the far side, Jeff let out a low whistle. Not far from the trail, nestled in a frame of forested mountains, sat the village. It reminded him more of an alpine Swiss village than anything else. The handsome houses were all two-storied and made of stone. The whole scene had a fairy tale look about it.

As they drew closer, a group of horsemen came racing out to greet them. Jeff's first thought was to turn and run, especially when he heard their yells.

"Don't run," laughed Dorje. "These are some of my relatives and friends coming to greet us."

When the group reached them, they found themselves surrounded by a bunch of happy, smiling, yelling men and boys on horseback. Right away, he could tell these people were different from the other Tibetans he had met since coming to this remote part of the world. While he certainly had liked the people he met, this group who rode out at breakneck speed to meet them was different. They were all dressed like Dorje; laughed, talked and did not seem at all shy; and each one was riding a fine looking horse. They were very open and friendly. The other Tibetans he met, although friendly, somehow seemed standoffish, shy, and almost afraid. Perhaps it was because of the Chinese. This group seemed very happy to see Dorje, and he was just as happy to see them.

"So these are some of Dorje's people. I am impressed," Jeff thought to himself.

After a while, Dorje raised his hand and said something in Tibetan. The group fell silent.

"This is my friend, Jeff," he said in English. "I will tell you just why he is here with me tonight when we will have a meeting."

The smiling faces now turned toward Jeff. "Welcome to our valley," they said almost in unison in English. He was surprised at how well they spoke the language. Dorje told him later that he began teaching the villagers English when he would return from school for a visit each year.

"They learn very fast," he said seriously, "and the children are taught English in our little village school," he added.

The group stopped in front of a very impressive three-storied house. "This," Dorje said with a sigh, "is my parents' house." As they dismounted, an elderly man and woman walked out to greet them.

"Dorje! Dorje!" they cried, wrapping their arms around him.

"These are my parents," Dorje said proudly to Jeff.

His father was tall—at least 6'5". He was a very imposing, ruggedly handsome figure of a man. They shook hands. His grip was warm and firm.

Dorje's mother was also tall. She held herself very erect, and her looks were even more appealing when she smiled, revealing her brilliant white teeth and dark, sparkling eyes. They both made Jeff feel very welcome, and they too spoke excellent English.

What Dorje's mother was wearing really caught Jeff's eye. She wore a gold embroidered, semi-cone shaped hat, a jacket with gold designs, and a skirt of some kind of cloth that looked as though it could have been made of gold thread. His father had on a fox fur hat, a rich silk jacket, gold and silver studded belt, with a silver-sheathed short sword and black corduroy pants tucked into high black leather boots. His hair was not braided in the usual Tibetan style, and his black curls fell almost to his shoulders. Like Dorje's mother, he smiled much; then all of the Tibetans Jeff had just met seemed to always be smiling. Like Dorje, his father was very athletic looking.

The ground floor of the house served as the stables. The second and third stories of the house were the living quarters and storage rooms. They reached the second story by climbing an outside stairway. The room they entered was very large, and the floor was covered with thick carpets. They sat in a circle on piles of rugs. The household help brought tea. Jeff was surprised that it was not the yak-buttered tea he had learned to drink. Instead, it was like the tea they had at home, and he was even given sugar. At first, it was difficult to see because of the room's dimness. When his eyes grew accustomed, he was almost overwhelmed by the richness of what he saw. The room was furnished as tastefully as any room in any mansion back home. There were rich woods and valuable looking tapestries, paintings and gold statues. All were beautiful works of art. He was speechless. He wondered how such treasures came to be in such a remote place. He was sure Dorje would answer his questions later. They talked of many things, the state of the world, and the problems in Tibet. Jeff was very impressed at just how knowledgeable both Dorje's parents were about the outside world. Then the food began to arrive. He was starving. This was not your normal Tibetan meal of tsampa, dried yak, and rancid yak-butter tea. This meal was a feast. The food was a combination of Chinese and Indian, with a little Western thrown in for good measure. He had never eaten so much or enjoyed a meal so much in his life.

When the help cleared everything away, Dorje's father suggested Dorje show Jeff around the village. He reminded them there was to be a meeting that night to discuss future plans.

They decided to walk rather than ride. The village was small, consisting of a few dozen large houses and several smaller ones. Everything had a spic-and-span look. There was no trash lying about, and the houses and few shops all had a well-cared-for appearance. It was all neat and tidy with a look of middle class prosperity. The people they met greeted Dorje like a long lost son. He was very happy and proud of the village and its friendly people. Most of the villagers seemed to speak good English. Only the very old spoke Tibetan when Jeff was introduced. Jeff asked about the fact that they had not seen any small children, but he just answered that they were in school and let the subject drop.

chapter 11

They walked for most of the afternoon. The sky was a deep blue with an occasional big, billowy white cloud scooting across as though it was being chased by something invisible. The rays of the warm sun were cooled by just the right breeze.

Jeff really wanted to know more about Dorje's parents, but really did not know how he should go about asking. Finally, he just blurted it out.

"Dorje, just what is the story about your parents? They don't seem to be sheltered from the rest of the world, and this valley is a long way from anything."

They were standing in the shade of a small grove of trees, and Dorje suggested they sit for a while. The place he chose was beneath the branches of a huge oak tree. A clear, cold stream ran just a few feet away. As they leaned their backs against the rough bark of the trunk, the sound of the stream, coupled with the rustling sound of the breeze through the leaves, was as pleasant a sound as anyone could ask for.

For several minutes, neither one said a word. Both were just too comfortable. They just sat and listened to the sounds of nature.

"This was probably just about as good as it ever gets," Jeff thought to himself. High above he could see a hawk, with its wings spread wide, circling in the sky. The entire world seemed at peace, but deep down inside, he knew it was not.

Finally, Dorje spoke. "I know you are very curious about my parents, this valley, and the people who live here," he began, "so, I am going to tell you. Some of it you have already been told, and I will be repeating myself, but this is all right. The whole story is going to take a little time, so just sit back and relax."

Jeff did not say a word. He sat hardly daring to breathe because he did not want to miss a word of what he was about to hear.

"Many years ago, my father ruled a large part of Tibet. He was a very powerful man and for that matter, still is. He is a prince. My mother, of course, is a princess. The area of Tibet he ruled over was one of the least populated but wealthiest provinces in Tibet. The people are Khambans, and the province is called Kham. They loved and respected my father and mother. When the Chinese invaded Tibet, it was the Khambans who fought the hardest against them. However, they had very inferior weapons, and many were killed. The Chinese knew about my father and wanted to capture him alive. He was too smart for them. He and many of his followers escaped to come here to this hidden valley. The Chinese have not the slightest clue that it even exists. As you already know, I was sent away to school. Whenever I was able to return, I would. On those occasions, my father had me teach English to the people here in the valley. I even set up a school, and my father sent some of the young adults to a special school in India to take a crash course in teaching. Of course, at first only a few subjects were taught, but now our small school is probably just about as good as any of its size anywhere."

"It seems to me," Jeff interrupted, "that the teachers have done a good job. There have only been a couple of the older people that I thought had a tough time speaking English. But the younger ones really seem to be up on things, especially about what's going on in the outside world. They certainly do not seem sheltered."

"My parents have traveled many times to many parts of the outside world and have sent the teachers to various countries to learn. Also, believe it or not, several newspapers are sent to the village. The news may be a little old by the time they get here, but not by much. My parents have a shortwave radio, and often many of the villagers will come and listen to programs. Actually, I think the people here are really up to date on the news of what is happening in the outside world."

"When your parents leave the valley to travel, how do they get out of here? They certainly cannot come and go the way we came in."

"No, you are right, they don't. My father has an agreement with the government of both Nepal and India. In return for information about what the Chinese army in Tibet is up to, they will fly in an unmarked helicopter to a small landing area not far out of the valley and pick up my parents any time they want to leave. And, of course, they will fly them back when they want to return. The route the helicopter flies is so far off the beaten path, no one ever sees it until it is just about to land. You might say that it just sneaks in the back door."

"Well, how can your father provide this information, and how do they get it in the first place?"

"Many years ago, he set up a spy system throughout Tibet. It is very efficient. Even today, the Chinese know nothing about it. Actually, that is how my father found out about your parents."

"How come you don't get to come and go by helicopter?"

"Even though this is among some of the most remote countries in the world, and the chance of the helicopter being seen, especially because of the route it flies to get here and back is very slight, it could happen. The Chinese, too, have spies all over Tibet. Anyway, neither my father nor the governments of both India and

Nepal want to take any extra chances, especially since my father is still wanted by the Chinese. But there have been rumors recently spread in the right places that he is dead. Hopefully the Chinese will fall for the rumor. However, there are special circumstances for which the helicopter will come. If, for instance, some special supplies are needed and it would take too long for one of our own caravans to go out and get them, the helicopter will fly them in. or for an emergency of some kind."

"Why did your father want the people here in this valley to learn to speak English?"

"Education has always been lacking in Tibet. He felt that if he could help his people in any way, it would be to give them as much education as possible. Not only have most of them learned to speak English, but many have learned to read both English and Tibetan. Before, only the Monks and the privileged few ever received any kind of education. The religion of Tibet is Buddhism. If a young boy was to get any kind of formal education, his parents had to place him in a monastery to become a monk. It is a very strict life."

"You are from a privileged background. Why were you sent out of the country for your education? Why didn't you go into a monastery?"

"The reason was so that in time I could set up a system of education here in this valley; a system for all ages, and this I have done. It was something I truly enjoyed doing. The thing that made the job even more rewarding was the desire of the people to learn—young, old, male, and female. For those younger who show they have the ability, when the time comes they are given a choice. If they want to further their education, they can go on to school either in India or Nepal. If someone turns out to be an exceptional student and shows great promise, they will almost certainly go on to a university or college."

"So just what are your father's plans? It sounds to me like he is trying to do as much for the people here in this valley as he can. What kind of future is there for them?"

"I do not know if I can really tell you exactly what he plans to do," Dorje replied, "but what I think he would like to do and hopes to do is to raise the standard of literacy at least here in this valley to the highest it can possibly be. He dreams that someday, the Chinese will leave Tibet. If that does ever happen, the people of this valley will be able, in a very big way, to help rebuild Tibet."

Since it was getting late, they decided it was time to head back to Dorje's house.

The evening meal was just as good as the one they ate earlier. Again, Jeff was so full he did not think he could get up to go to the next room, where the heads of the village were to have their meeting.

The room was lit by several small yak-butter lamps. Their flickering glow added an eerie effect to the surroundings.

They were all seated in a semicircle with Dorje's father at the middle. Jeff sat next to Dorje, who in turn sat on his father's right. Tea was served, and Jeff was asked if he would rather have regular tea. Because he had begun to like the Tibetan tea, he chose to have that which brought a nod of approval from several of the Tibetans. About halfway through the meeting, Jeff began to feel sick. It started with a headache, and then his whole body began to ache. One minute he would be hot, and the next he would be cold. His head began to swim, and the last thing he remembered was telling Dorje he really felt lousy. When he tried to stand, he collapsed into a heap on the floor. The nearest medical doctor was hundreds of miles and many days away. What they did was call in the village doctor who was a Buddhist monk. Even in far-off Tibet, it takes many years of intense study to become their kind of doctor. When the monk first looked at Jeff, he told Dorje and his parents he felt there was little hope for his recovery, but he would try.

If the monk was not at his side, giving him his home made

medicines, someone else was. Never was Jeff left alone. For five days and nights, he teetered on the edge of death. He could not see the looks of grave concern on the faces of Dorje, his parents, and the others who attended him. He could not know their feelings of helplessness as they saw his suffering. One minute he was burning with fever, throwing off any blankets that were covering him. The next minute, he would be begging for more covers because he was freezing.

All of a sudden he would sit up and scream for help with his eyes in a glazed state because of the pain and fever. He would begin thrashing uncontrollably, throwing his arms wildly into the air. It would take at least three people to hold him down. On the fifth day, the monk said if his condition did not improve by the next day that soon he would surely die.

It was then, when Jeff was at the most dangerous point in his illness, that a runner arrived. The runner worked in the monastery where his parents were being held captive and was one of Dorje's father's spies. The message the runner brought said that most of Colonel Chin's men would be leaving within a month for some kind of special training. Probably only a skeleton crew would be left at the monastery.

It was after midnight when Jeff began to show a slight improvement. By morning, he was drinking tea, and by evening, he wanted food and lots of it. The whole household was elated. The monk said what he felt had saved Jeff's life was that he was young and in very good physical condition.

Although he was still very weak, the next morning with help, Jeff was able to take a short walk around the room.

When Dorje told him about the delay to try to free his parents and the reason why, Jeff was thrilled. It would give him time to get back his strength so he would be able to go with them.

The monk was very pleased when he came to see Jeff a few days after he was back on his feet. He told Jeff, in halting English, he was very happy he was doing so well, and that he was fortunate to have survived his illness. Jeff, in turn, thanked not only the monk but everyone else for all they had done for him. He was very grateful.

The monk was very old and bent. He stood no more than five feet tall. Standing on his tiptoes he patted Jeff on the head and said, "You are very welcome."

Jeff began to spend his days out in the fresh air, soaking up the warm sun and walking; just short distances at first. Often he had to sit and rest, but after the first few days he was walking much farther. With each new day he could feel his body getting stronger and stronger. Jeff really enjoyed his walks.

Occasionally, Dorje would go with him. Mostly, though, he would go alone because Dorje was busy, involved in various village projects. Because the valley was so beautiful and was full of all kinds of wildlife—both animals and birds—he never grew bored. In fact, it was just the opposite. He could hardly wait to get out and often left in the early morning, only to return near dark. He would take some food, and there was always either a cold, crystal-clear stream or spring close by where he could quench his thirst. It was a paradise. After several days of this kind of exercise, Jeff felt like his old self.

One morning before Jeff left on his walk, Dorje told him his father wanted to see both of them that night after the evening meal. Jeff did not ask why, and Dorje did not tell him, but he felt a twinge of excitement all the same.

Jeff, Dorje, and Dorje's father sat and drank tea. His father remarked on how well Jeff looked and asked if he felt as strong as he did before he became ill.

"Yes sir," Jeff replied firmly. "I feel as good right now as I did the day we got here."

"That's wonderful," he said, "because I have something very

important to tell you, but not right now. I have called a meeting for tomorrow night, and I would like you to attend."

A large grin of satisfaction crossed Jeff's face. He thought to himself that it looked like things might be about to happen. Why would Dorje's father call another meeting and ask him to attend if they weren't?

That night, Jeff did not sleep well at all. He had a very strange dream. When he awoke from the dream, he felt as exhausted as if he had finished running a marathon race. It was a dream the likes of which he had never before experienced.

He was in the mountains, probably somewhere in the Himalayas. He was alone, walking on a very narrow and dangerous trail that tightly hugged the side of a very steep cliff. It was windy, cold, and dark. He kept stumbling because the trail was very uneven and littered with rocks. Several times, he almost fell over the edge into the depths of a seemingly bottomless canyon. Suddenly, it began to rain. There were ear-shattering claps of thunder and blinding flashes of lightening. A violent wind began to roar down the canyon. The roar of the wind, periodic crashes of thunder, and blinding flashes of lightening were almost unbearable. Without any warning, a boulder the size of a small house came ricocheting down the mountainside, barely missing him. His knees and legs felt like rubber. He was so exhausted he was about ready to give up. When he had just about made up his mind to lie down, never to get up again, something came over him. It was a strange kind of power that seemed to creep over his body, giving him just enough strength to keep struggling forward. Rounding a sharp bend, through the driving rain he could just barely make out a dim light in the distance.

An extra brilliant sheet of lightening flashed across the sky, lighting up the landscape as though it was a sunny, summer day. In that short time, he saw a building that looked like it might be a house. This was where the light was coming from. He staggered and stumbled forward as fast as his weakened legs would carry him. He knew he had to reach that light. The closer he got, the brighter the light seemed to glow. When he was finally close enough, he reached out to grab the handle of the front door, only to have the whole building move just out of his reach. Again and again it happened. Every time he got close enough to reach the handle, the building would move. It seemed to be teasing him . . . testing him. Jeff knew he had to keep trying. He had to get inside that house. Sheer willpower was all that kept him on his feet.

Finally, mustering all the strength he had left in his body, he made one last try. This time he was able to grab onto the door's handle. It would not turn. The door, when he pushed on it, would not budge. He began to knock, but the sound of his feeble tapping was lost in the howling of the wind. From weakness, he sank to his knees. He screamed in desperation as a loud peal of thunder bounced and echoed off the sides of the canyon walls.

"One more time," he muttered with determination in his voice. This time the door opened. Inside was what looked to be a bright, warm, comfortable room. It looked exactly like their living room back home. The furniture was the same. Over by the far wall sat an old upright piano, just like the one at home.

What he did not notice at first were both of his parents sitting where they would normally sit, close to each other on the sofa next to the fireplace. When he looked at them, they both gave him a warm smile but did not say anything. It was at that point the dream ended and he awoke.

He was puzzled, very puzzled. He felt the dream was trying to tell him something, but what? He lay for a long time trying to figure it out. It was just as the sun was rising, and Jeff was getting up when he felt he had found the answer. He knew what the dream was trying to tell him, and he knew that now, more than ever, he would do everything within his power to be a part of freeing his parents.

chapter 12

It was a beautiful, crystal-clear morning. After breakfast, Jeff went for his usual walk. There was just so much to see. Not only were the walks good for him, but each day he seemed to discover something new. Never had he seen or been in a place of such beauty and where the people seemed totally content and happy.

He sat on a grassy bank above a stream to eat his lunch. A large tree gave him plenty of shade from the hot sun. Looking down into the deep, clear pool just below where he sat, he let out a sudden, "Wow . . . trout. I can't believe it."

Now, if there was anything that really got him excited, it was trout, especially trout in a stream. He loved to fly fish for trout more than anything else. He even learned to tie his own flies. It was his dad who had taught him to fish and tie flies. It was the one thing they had in common. They used to fish the little river near their town. As he gazed into the pool, he could see several nice trout lazily swimming near the bottom. Occasionally, one would rise ever so slowly and gently sip in a floating insect, leaving a series of rings spreading across the almost glass-like surface of the water.

"If only I had my fly rod," he said with longing in his voice.

But the rod, along with the rest of his fishing equipment, was many thousands of miles away, back home in his room. When he thought about it, he did not know why he hadn't seen trout in the other streams he visited in the valley. He guessed it was because he had too much on his mind and was not really looking.

"Wait just a minute," he exclaimed, slapping his hands together. "I do know where there are some fish hooks. When I bought that survival kit in that war surplus store to bring with me, I remember seeing a small plastic envelope with at least a dozen fish hooks in it."

The wheels in his brain began to turn.

"I think," he said, still talking aloud to himself, "I think I can gather up enough chicken feathers and the other stuff I need to tie up some flies, but what about a rod and fly line and leaders?"

He had been pacing up and down, deep in thought, but now he sat heavily on a nearby log. Leaning forward, his hands on his chin, he felt a sense of despair. Again, the wheels in his brain began to turn. Willows . . . there were plenty of willow growing along the streams in the valley. What he needed was a nice straight piece of willow about eight feet long. Not too big around at the butt end, tapering down to a fairly fine tip, and with plenty of backbone for strength. He thought he could obtain some kind of twine that might work as a fly line, but what about leaders. Aha, horsehair! He knew from reading that in the old days they made their leaders out of horsehair. There were certainly plenty of horses in the valley. What he wanted, though, was hair from a horse whose tail was of a very light color.

Immediately, he began to search for a suitable piece of willow. Much to his surprise, it was not long before he found a branch that he thought might just work. After trimming off all of the access leaves and branches, he was really pleased and felt he had just what he wanted.

While hurrying back to the village with his new rod, another idea flashed into his head. He stopped at the small shop that served, among other things, as the village blacksmith. He had been introduced to its owner when they first arrived, so he knew the man spoke good English.

"I would like to know," asked Jeff, "if you could make me some short pieces of wire. I want to use them to make round guides to place on this willow pole so that I can run string through them. I will need about ten or twelve."

The blacksmith nodded his head. He said it would be no problem to make what Jeff wanted. The blacksmith told him to come back later in the day and they would be ready.

Next, Jeff visited a village woman who made cloth. She had plenty of heavy twine and gave him as much as he thought he might need. The thread she offered he would use to wrap the guides the blacksmith made for him onto the willow pole. The thread was also just right to use when he tied his flies. The several strands of wool in various colors were just what he needed to wrap on the shank of the hook to make the body of the flies.

"Now," he thought to himself, "what I need is some long strands of hair from the tail of the lightest colored horse I can find. But how do I go about finding one? Ah," he said, tapping the side of his head, "what better person to ask than the blacksmith."

After killing some time, that was just where he headed . . . back to the blacksmith.

"Yes," the blacksmith answered, "your wires are ready." When Jeff asked if he knew where there might be a certain color horse, he said he just happened to have a light gray stallion. When Jeff wanted to know if by chance the horse had a long light-colored tail, he answered that it did. The man told Jeff if he would like to see the horse he would show it to him. The animal was in an enclosure just out behind his shop, and he could have as many strands of hair from the tail as he wanted.

"However," he warned, shaking his head, "I will have to hold the horse for you while you try to get what you need."

It was a beautiful animal. Its body was a light gray, with an almost pure white mane and tail. It was just the color Jeff needed. He could certainly see why it would take the both of them to get what he needed. This was one wild horse. It nervously pawed the ground with its front hooves and snorted with fire in its eyes. As they got closer, a change came over the animal. It stopped its trembling and pawing and actually became calm.

"That is very strange," the blacksmith said in a puzzled voice. "This horse really does not like or trust people at all. Look at him . . . I have never seen him so quiet. The only reason I can get close to him or ride him is because I feed him. No one but me has ever been able to touch him." He continued, "I raised him from a colt and have taken great pains to try to gain his trust. I got him from some nomads, and I'm sure they mistreated him. Look, just look—he is actually letting you pet him."

"Then you are able to ride him?" questioned Jeff.

"Yes, but I have other mounts I would rather ride. I am getting old, and he is a lot of horse to handle. My other horses are all out to pasture. He is kept here at the back of my shop because he might cause trouble with the other horses."

"He looks like he might be a fairly fast horse. Is he?"

"I don't like to brag, but we here in the valley hold several races among ourselves each year. They are very popular, and many horses are entered. This horse has never been beaten, and he has raced against the finest in the valley. Our horses are probably some of the best, if not the best, in all of Tibet. He has even beaten Dorje's fastest horse. Dorje is like a son to me. I would like for him to have the animal, and as good as he is with horses, he is the first to admit that he is not able to handle him."

"Does he have a name?"

"No. I have never named him. Do not ask me why, because I do not know."

"Well, he has got to have a name," stated Jeff as he continued to pet the horse. "Would it be all right with you if I named him?"

"Certainly," replied the blacksmith, "but what name did you have in mind?"

"Well, he is such a strong, beautiful, spirited, and intelligent looking animal, I kind of thought Hercules would be a good name."

"A worthy name for a worthy horse," answered the blacksmith with a nod of his head.

"How did you know about Hercules?" Jeff asked respectfully.

"Many years ago, I lived and went to school in India. Among other things, I studied ancient history. I quickly tired of life in civilization. So, after I finished my studies, I returned to Tibet and here to this valley to be with Dorje's father. We have been friends since childhood. It was a decision I have never regretted. I was one of those with Dorje's father when he discovered the valley. That was a very long time ago. Anyway, it seems as though Hercules has really taken a liking to you. Would you like to ride him?"

"Would I," came Jeff's rather nervous reply. "But do you think he would let me?"

"With the way he has been behaving with you standing next to him . . . well, if I am any judge of horses, I would say you are the only person other than myself who he would allow to get on his back."

At that instant, Hercules began to nuzzle his nose against Jeff's arm.

"Just look at him. I have never seen this horse show any kind of affection toward anyone or anything. I have been told you are a good rider, but let me tell you, if you do ride Hercules, you will find he is the smoothest gated horse you have ever ridden. He truly is a wonderful animal. I know he would let you ride him, but that will have to be another time. As soon as you get what you want, I must get back to work."

It took only a minute for Jeff to cut as many hairs from Hercules's tail as he thought he might need. The horse did not even budge while he was doing it. He thanked the blacksmith, saying he would indeed like to ride Hercules, and he would be back another time soon.

Now, Jeff had all of the various things he needed to make what he felt would be at least a functional fly-fishing outfit.

First, he would assemble the rod and then fashion the line and make the horsehair leaders. This little project would take a bit of time. When he was finished and if he felt he really did have something functional, then he would try to find rooster feathers. He wanted the neck feathers or hackles from a rooster because they tended to be stiffer than those from a hen. You need stiff hackles when tying dry flies. The stiffness makes the fly float on the surface of the water much better than a softer hen feather or hackle, which tends to soak up water much faster, thus causing the fly to sink. These softer web feathers are used in tying wet flies. Wet flies are tied to sink beneath the water's surface. These hackles imitate the legs of the insect, and stiff hackles are also used for the tail of the fly.

Sitting under a tree, his back against its trunk for support, he began to work. First he made the guides out of the wire. Next, at various intervals along the length of the pole, he wrapped each guide securely in place with thread. Then he started on the leader. First he braided three strands of horsehair so there was a loop at the top part. This was where the heavy twine he would be using for the fly line would attach to the leader. This braiding was a bit tricky and took some time. To this two-foot section, he tied two strands of about the same length. For the last part of the leader, he used one strand of hair about three-feet long. When he pulled on it, he was very surprised at just how strong a single strand of horsehair was. Plenty strong enough, he felt, to land even a good-sized trout.

"A very satisfactory leader if I do say so myself," he said rather smugly.

It was when he had finished connecting the line to the leader that he realized he did not have a reel on which to put the line.

"How stupid," he thought aloud. "Oh, well, I'll just make do and use my left arm as the reel. I'll wrap the line around my left hand, and with a little practice, I should not have any trouble at all."

He knew with his makeshift equipment he would not be able to cast the fly like he normally would. Instead, he would use the technique called dapping, just like they use to do in the days before reels. When you dap, you hold the rod tip out over the water with just enough line out so that when you drop the tip of the rod, it causes the fly to light on the water just like a living insect. Then you let it float over the fish or where a fish might be, and if you are lucky, one will take it. When he finished, he went back to Dorje's parents' house. He asked Dorje if he knew where he could get the rooster feathers he needed to tie his flies.

"If what you want are chicken feathers," he said, "I can take you where you can get as many as you want and in all colors."

"That's great! When can we go?"

"Not until tomorrow morning. Even though it is not very far, it's getting too late. You do remember my father wants you to attend the meeting tonight."

"Well, no," Jeff hesitantly answered, "but it did almost slip my mind. I guess I got a little overexcited about fishing."

"That's understandable," sympathized Dorje. "I think you really need to do some fishing. It would certainly help keep your mind occupied. That in itself will make the waiting much easier. Who knows, perhaps tonight we will find out just when we are going to try to free your parents. My father has not even told me exactly why he has called this meeting. Now, though, it is just about time for the evening meal."

It was then that Jeff realized just how hungry he was, and he really outdid himself at dinner. He knew whenever he ate like that at home, his mother always accused him of having a bottomless pit for a stomach.

That evening at the meeting, seated with the others he had grown to know and respect, he had the feeling he was really a part of them. They even began to treat him like one of their own.

The meeting, as before, was conducted in English. It lasted quite a long time, and many subjects were discussed. The last, and most important, was Jeff's parents.

"One of our friends who works in the monastery," began Dorje's father, "has sent word that there has been a slight delay in the departure of Colonel Chin's men. It should only be a week, maybe two at most. All must be ready at a moment's notice. I wish I were able to go, but I am not as young as I used to be."

This last statement brought a number of smiles to the faces of those seated in the circle. To the men, they remembered how brave their leader had been in those early years of struggle against the Chinese invaders.

"The rescue party," he continued, "will be led by Dorje, who as you know has been well trained. No guns will be taken. I do not want any shooting. Of course, swords and daggers will be carried. They will not be coming straight back here. We certainly do not want to take the chance the Chinese would be able to follow them and find our valley. Instead, when they leave the monastery, they will travel on trails leading away from here. Eventually they will be able to circle around and come in by our escape route. We do have a trick or two in mind to help them throw the soldiers off their trail. Only the least amount of food for each man will be carried, plus some extra for Jeff's parents. They must travel as light as they can; the lighter, the better. Of course, they will go by horse, and two extra mounts will be taken. I have been told both his parents are excellent riders. The rescue party must get in and out of the monastery just as quickly as possible. They must act quietly and swiftly if they are to accomplish their goal. They will be met at the prearranged time at the front entrance to the monastery by one of our people who will let them in. As it looks now, the best time to try to release the Thorntons is going to be around midnight. That seems to be when they are sure to be in their sleeping quarters and least guarded. Hopefully things will not change. One thing I almost forgot to tell you is when Colonel Chin leaves with his troops, he will be taking the helicopter. As you know, we, as a group, have chosen four men to go with Dorje and Jeff. If all goes well, two will be added to that figure when they get back to our valley."

Those last words especially sent a chill down Jeff's spine. "It seems forever since I last saw them," he thought sadly to himself. "I just hope everything goes according to plan."

When the meeting was over and they were all drinking a last cup of tea, Dorje took Jeff aside.

"I can tell by the look on your face," he began with a note of sympathy in his voice, "that you are very worried about whether we can free your parents. From now until it is time to leave will be a very stressful time for you. So I suggest you do as much fishing and anything else you choose to keep your mind occupied. It will make the time go by much faster. And," he added after a short pause, "we will free your parents."

"Thanks, Dorje, I really appreciate all you are doing. And I will certainly take your advice about keeping busy."

The next morning after breakfast, Dorje took Jeff to what must have been some kind of small chicken farm. There were chickens all over the place in pens, running loose, and several were even perched in the lower branches of a tree.

"What is this place," he asked, "some kind of chicken farm way off in one of the most remote parts of Tibet? I have never seen so many chickens in my life. I can hardly believe it."

At that very instant, one of the roosters in the tree decided to take off in its chicken like fluttering flight and land on Jeff's shoulder. You talk about being surprised. He almost became airborne. They both had a good laugh. It turned out the rooster was very tame and was one of the colors he needed for his flies. The chicken very obligingly held still while Jeff plucked several feathers from its neck. As he examined the feathers, he told Dorje the fiber of the feathers was very stiff. It was perfect for tying dry flies.

"With all of the excitement, I almost forgot to answer your question. The lady who has all of these chickens is a widow. Her husband was killed many years ago fighting the Chinese. She did not want to take any kind of charity from the villagers, so she decided to go into the chicken and egg business. It was agreed by all the villagers to obtain their eggs from her and not to raise chickens themselves. Since it was such a small village, it seems to have worked out very well. It is just another one of the ways the people here look after each other."

As they stood talking, the woman came out of her small, well-kept house. When she saw Dorje, her wrinkled face broke into a broad smile. Even though she was bent over with age, she moved with surprising quickness to his side. She wrapped her arms around his waist and gave him a warm hug. Dorje began speaking to her in Tibetan, but she told him in quite good English to speak to her in that language.

"When," he said with astonishment, "did you learn to speak English?"

"After the last time you were here, I decided it was time I learned. I went to the classes the school teacher was giving for us old people and now, I speak it fairly good."

"That's great, and yes, you really do speak it good. I am very proud of you. Do you remember when I tried to get you to learn and you said you were too old? Well, it looks like you were wrong," he kidded.

"It was not easy," she answered, waving a finger in his face teasingly, "but I worked very hard. I would not even let myself think in Tibetan, only in English. I hate to admit it, but I do wish I had begun learning when you wanted me to. Now, what has brought you here, Dorje?"

"Well," he began as he introduced Jeff, "my friend here needs some feathers from some of your roosters."

"If that is what your friend wants," she answered matter of factually, "all he has to do is tell me which roosters to catch and I will catch them."

It was, as she said, just as simple as that. When he pointed out a rooster of the color he wanted some feathers from, she would just walk up to the bird, pick it up, and hold it so he could pull out as many from each as he thought he might need. Not a single bird struggled in any way. They seemed to be as tame as a domestic dog or cat, and she had a name for each. After they were finished and had thanked her and were just about to leave, she told them to wait just a minute. When she returned she said, "I thought you might like these," and handed Dorje a basket full of fresh eggs.

Jeff began tying flies as soon as they returned to Dorje's house. Since he did not have a fly tying vise to hold the hook, he had to improvise and use his fingers. At first he was clumsy and was not at all satisfied with the results, so he took the flies apart and started over. He found that with just a little more practice he began to get the hang of it, and the patterns he turned out were not half bad. He ended up by tying a whole dozen—four each in different color combinations.

"Not bad, not bad," he said, patting himself on the back. "Now if the trout will only cooperate."

By the time he was finished and had cleaned the mess he made, it was time for lunch. He thought instead of eating with Dorje, he would take some food with him and eat by the stream. Before he left, he told Dorje about visiting the blacksmith and naming Hercules.

"A fine horse," Dorje told him. "I hope you are able to ride him because I certainly was not. The blacksmith can, but even he has a hard time, and he is certainly the finest rider in the valley."

"What I think I will do," said Jeff more to himself than Dorje, "is go now and ask the blacksmith if I can ride Hercules. If he gives the okay, then I'll ride him to the places I want to fish. I was going to walk, but I'm fully recovered from my sickness, and it would probably be a good idea to get back in the saddle again. Besides," he added, "I certainly remember how saddle sore I was when we first got to the valley. This way I can at least get used to riding. Besides, I can surely cover a lot more ground and explore a lot more water by horseback. I know I could ride one of your horses, but Hercules really seemed to take a liking to me and trusted me. And, I've got to admit, I really like that horse."

He asked one of the people who worked in the house if they could give him something in which to carry his things. After a little searching, he handed him a large, soft leather pouch with a shoulder strap.

"Plenty big enough for what I need. Big enough even for my lunch and anything else I can get into it. Just the right thing," he said and thanked them.

He went straight to the blacksmiths.

"I am very pleased that you have asked to ride Hercules. It is just what the horse needs, and if I know anything about horses, from the way you two got along, I am sure you will not have any kind of trouble when you ride him. Let's just have you ride him around the back here first, just to make sure."

They walked out back to where Hercules was kept. The big

horse actually acted as though he was glad to see Jeff. When he reached out to pet him, the horse gave a soft sound and nuzzled him with his nose.

The horse stood absolutely still while the blacksmith saddled and bridled him. He did not even stomp a hoof. When he finished, the blacksmith said he had never seen the animal so at ease.

"What you do to this horse I cannot figure out," said the blacksmith in a puzzled tone. "You hold some kind of spell over him."

Hercules then began to lightly stomp his hooves as though he was anxious to get on the trail, so Jeff rather nervously decided it was time to mount up. He need not have worried because once in the saddle, he walked the horse in a circle a few times to get the feel of how to handle him. Next, he asked to have the gate opened so he could ride out a short distance, but he wanted the blacksmith to stand by just in case he needed him. He had thought Dorje's horse was the finest he had ever ridden—that was until now.

As a kid, watching the old cowboy movies on the television, he was always thrilled by the unusually fine horse ridden by the "good guy" in the movie. "Hercules," he thought to himself with pride, "would put any of those horses to shame." He could not help thinking what a remarkable animal Hercules really was.

The big horse followed Jeff's commands as though he was actually anticipating them. Mostly, though, Jeff let the horse have his head. After several minutes, he turned and trotted the horse to where the blacksmith was standing. After dismounting, he asked if Hercules had any kind of training.

"No," came his firm reply. "As I told you, I got him from some nomads who I am sure treated him very badly. I have only ridden him in some races. He just seems to be one of those rare animals that when he takes to someone, he'll do anything asked of him. And it looks like you are the lucky one he has placed his trust in."

Jeff asked the blacksmith if he would hand him his leather bag. Next, he asked if he would please tie his fishing rod to two leather straps hanging from the saddle. When he did, this made it look like a long radio antenna sticking up in the air, but at the moment that was the best they could do. The blacksmith told him that later he might be able to fix up something to make it easier to carry his pole, but for now, this would have to suffice.

Jeff slung the leather bag over his shoulder and waved goodbye. They were off to the trail, and the way the large animal was acting, he was as excited as Jeff to finally be on their way.

"What a great afternoon," Jeff said a little too loud, because the horse did give a bit of a lurch. A pat on the neck soon settled him down.

Hercules did not want to walk, so Jeff let him break into a nice, easy trot. The smoothness and speed of his trot caused Jeff to admire Hercules even more, and he knew they were in for a wonderful afternoon. It was at that exact moment, the horse began to shake his head as though he was in total agreement.

Jeff chose to begin by fishing in the stream where he first saw the trout. With Hercules's speed, it was not long before they reached their destination. After dismounting, he led Hercules to a small grove of trees where he would be in the shade, tethered him, and removed the saddle. There was plenty of grass for him to munch. The horse heaved a big sigh and nuzzled his large nose against Jeff's chest, telling him he liked the spot Jeff chose.

It took a little while and a bit of doing, but finally he had his equipment set up. Carefully, he tied on one of his flies to the end of the horsehair leader, using the same knot he would have used if he were fishing with a regular leader.

"Wow," he exclaimed, "this horsetail ties a pretty darned good knot."

He was really pleased as he examined and pulled on the knot to see just how strong it was.

"Heck, this stuff is strong enough to land a pretty big fish; certainly one bigger than any I have ever caught."

Clumps of willows dotted Jeff's side of the stream. The opposite bank was fairly free of any kind of growth other than the overhanging long meadow grass. It seemed to Jeff to be the ideal kind of setting for dapping. There was even a gentle breeze blowing upstream.

With everything set up, he was ready to go. Cautiously, ever so cautiously, he crept to a small clump of willows at the edge of the stream. The willows would shield him from the fish. Peering over the edge of the rather high bank into the gently flowing current, he saw several nice trout lazily swimming in the crystal-clear depths of the pool. He noticed several insects floating on the water's surface. There would be a gentle sip, and an insect would disappear. All that would be left were the telltale rings caused by the fish when it sucked in the insect. It was difficult to describe, but only dyed-in-the-wool fisherman would have felt the thrill of seeing those fish rise, and Jeff was certainly experiencing that thrill.

"Take it easy, take it easy," he whispered to himself. "Just ease the rod out over the water just a few feet below the closest fish. The breeze should do the rest."

The breeze caught the six or seven foot of line that Jeff fed out. When he judged the fly to be a few feet in front of the trout, he lowered the rod tip, causing the fly to land softly on the surface. After a few seconds of twirling around in a slight whirlpool, it was caught by the current and began to float, lifelike, downstream. Jeff watched as a trout raised itself slowly to the surface to intercept what it thought to be a live insect. He held his breath. Would the fly keep on floating in a natural way? Or would it suddenly start to float in an unnatural manner, causing the fish to realize that it was not a tasty mouthful but something it should shy away from. Closer and closer came the fish until it was poised just beneath the feathered imitation. The big fish really seemed to be giving it the once over. Then, for no apparent reason, the fish gave a slight wag of its broad tail and sank back into the depths of the pool and its original position.

"That fish must be well over twenty inches long," Jeff, moaned aloud. He brought the fly back to his hand so he could check it out.

"Well, I'll be darned," he said with a wry grin on his sun-tanned face, "these fish have probably never been fished for, but they are sure not stupid." He then pulled a small piece of grass off the point of the hook. A lesson was learned. From then on, he would check out the hook before he tried for a fish, just to make sure there was nothing wrong.

He decided instead of moving to another part of the stream, he would wait and fish this pool again after he let it rest. Perhaps he could get the big fish to rise again. Only this time, there would not be anything on the hook to make the trout think it was not a real insect. The wait might help to settle him down, as well.

Jeff sat in the cool shade, his back resting against the trunk of a large tree. He would have been totally at peace with the world had it not been for the horrible feeling he always carried because of the predicament his parents were in. He began to think about Trudy and home. He hoped she was not too worried. When he had asked Dorje if it would be possible to send a letter, he said yes, and he would send it out with the next helicopter.

"Do you know when that might be?"

"It just so happens it will be within the next few days. There is a shipment of goods coming in from India. So give me the letter when you write it and I'll make sure it gets mailed. It should not take more than a week for it to get to your friend."

That very night, Jeff wrote Trudy a long letter telling her about much of what had happened. One of the things he really made a point of telling her was how beautiful the valley was and how friendly the people who lived there were. Some of it would sound pretty farfetched to her, but Trudy would know he would only tell her the truth.

When he gave the letter to Dorje, Dorje told Jeff that the pilot would be given strict instructions to mail it as soon as possible. This made Jeff feel a lot better. For a long time he had been feeling guilty about not writing to let her know he was fine. He knew, though, she would understand.

His daydreaming brought back the memory when he and his dad began to teach Trudy how to fly fish and the excitement they all felt when she caught her first trout. She caught on very quickly and seemed to love it just as much as he and his dad. She even wanted to learn to tie her own flies. He was the first to admit that at fly tying, she was much better than he. Yes, Trudy tied beautiful flies.

"Well," he said as he stood and stretched, "I think it's been plenty long enough. Now maybe I can fool that fish into taking my fly."

He worked his way back into position. The gentle breeze was still blowing, and he could still see several trout where they lay, hugging the bottom of the pool. The fly touched the water's surface as lightly as a thistle. It floated only a short way before it was intercepted by what looked to be the same fish that earlier had refused the fly. There was a slurping sound as the fish sucked in the fly.

Jeff struck and immediately felt the pull of a heavy fish. Even though his adrenaline was really pumping, he did not strike too hard. If he had, the delicate horsehair leader would have broken for sure. The fish was well hooked, and what a fish it was. It jumped; it ran all around the pool; it flopped on the surface, and jumped again and again. This trout knew every trick in the book, plus a few of its own to get free. Even though his equipment was makeshift, Jeff fought the fish with a skill that even surprised him.

Finally the fish lay on its side just beneath the surface, too tired to move. Carefully, ever so carefully, Jeff led the fish to his hand to examine it.

"What a beautiful brown trout," he said with admiration in his voice.

He could see where the fly was solidly embedded in the side of the fish's mouth. Very gently he reached down and worked the fly loose. He was glad he had bent the barb on the hook down because it made removing the fly from the fish a lot easier. Once the fly was out, he held the trout under the water so it was facing upstream and began to slowly move it back and forth, giving it artificial respiration. It was not long before he felt a surge of energy travel through the fish, and it began to struggle to regain its freedom. Jeff knew the fish was ready.

After he took his hands away, for a few seconds the trout did not make a move. Then, sensing it was free, it shattered the surface with its huge tail and swam quickly back to the safety of the bottom of the pool.

Jeff felt good. In fact, he could not remember when he had felt so good.

After drying the fly and fluffing it back into shape, he decided to work his way upstream fishing all the likely places as he went. It was not long before he felt he was really getting the hang of how to handle his equipment. The hardest thing to do, he found, was to work the rod with just the right amount of line out so the fly would land on the water somewhat close to where he wanted it. The wind certainly had a lot to do with this and would often either quit blowing all together or become suddenly stronger just at the wrong time. It was not long before he was taking this in stride.

Working his way slowly upstream, he managed to land and release several more trout. Even though none were quite as big as the first, they were all very hard fighting fish.

Suddenly it dawned on him he had not eaten since early that morning and was hungry. He was so hungry, it felt as though his stomach was poking into his backbone.

He retraced his steps back downstream to where he had tethered Hercules. The big horse let out a snort and began to shake his head when he saw Jeff, as if to show he was happy to see him.

After giving the horse a handful of dried fruit as a treat, Jeff found the perfect spot under a tree to have his lunch. The meadow grass was so thick it almost felt like a soft cushion. After eating the generous lunch that was given him, he felt a little sleepy. Since it was the middle of the day and normally not the best time to fish, he thought he would take a nap.

As he was drifting off to sleep, he had the same feeling he had the night he went to meet Dorje—the night Captain Ling was following him. He was so sleepy he really did not pay much attention to the way he felt. He was sleepy and all he wanted to do was take a nap—a nice, long nap.

How long he slept he did not know, but he only awoke because Hercules was making one heck of a racket. The big horse was stomping his hooves, snorting, whinnying, and shaking his head. When Jeff reached his side, he could see fear in his eyes. He had a really hard time trying to calm him down. It took several minutes of soothing talk and petting. Even when he finally stood still, his whole body was shaking, and fear was still in his eyes. It was when things finally did calm down that Jeff thought he heard a noise in the thick bushes not too far away. Was it a rustling of the leaves caused by the wind? Was it his imagination? The only way to find out was go and have a look around.

He thought he had checked out the area pretty well and found nothing unusual. He was just about to head back to where Hercules was when he just happened to glance down at the ground. What he saw in a small patch of soft dirt caused his heart to skip a beat.

chapter 13

Jeff was frightened. He ran back to Hercules as fast as he could. He hurriedly grabbed his equipment, jumped into the saddle, and let the horse have its head all the way back to the village.

He reined Hercules to a sliding stop in front of Dorje's parents' house, dismounted and ran up the stairs. He bumped into Dorje, who was coming out just as he was about to burst through the front door.

"Have you got a few minutes?" Jeff pleaded. "I've got something to tell you that just can't wait."

"Sure. I was on my way to the school, but by the look on your face, the school can wait. First, though, calm down. Take it easy and then tell me all about it."

After a few false starts, Jeff was able to begin telling Dorje about what he had seen in the dirt. It was probably because he was still rattled that he actually began his story by telling about the trout he caught. Dorje listened patiently. Finally, he got to the part where Hercules woke him from his nap.

"He really was frightened about something, and I really had a hard time calming him down. When I had him quiet, I thought I heard something in the bushes. They were quite thick, so I really could not see far. I decided to have a look. I did not see a thing, and I was ready to head back, when I happened to look down at the ground. That's when I saw it in a small patch of dirt."

He began to get excited again, so Dorje told him to take a few deep breaths and then continue with his story.

"What I saw," he said, forcing himself to talk slowly, "was the largest, bare, human footprint I have ever seen in my life, right there in the dirt. I saw it just as plain as I see you standing in front of me. I thought at first it was from some kind of very big animal, but this print was not from any animal. It was human. I don't know what kind of human made it, but it was definitely a human footprint. The scary thing about the print was its size. Whoever or whatever made it has to be at least ten feet tall. It was huge."

At that point Dorje took Jeff and led him by the arm to a room where they could be alone. Dorje wanted to make sure they could talk without being interrupted.

"Sit down, Jeff, and listen very carefully to what I am about to tell you. It is going to sound stranger than anything you have ever heard or have been told in your whole life. It happened many years ago, before I was born. My father was being relentlessly hunted by the Chinese. They wanted very badly to capture him because of the strong influence and respect he had from the Tibetan people. Twice they came close to catching him, but each time he was warned and able to slip away. He knew he had to find a place, a safe place, where he did not have to worry about being captured. Not only for himself and my mother, but for what was left of his Khamban followers. Many, you see, had been killed by the Chinese. But where was such a place? There seemed to be nowhere safe from the Chinese, even in a country as large and rugged as Tibet.

"Then, one day, he and three of those closest to him met a monk who was very old and dying. He told them about a valley he had stumbled onto when, as a young man, he was on his way to a distant monastery. While traveling, he became lost. He wandered around for days, trying to find his way. It was during that time, and just by chance, he stumbled onto this valley. His memory was not very good, but he was able to tell my father just about where he thought it might be. Though his directions were sketchy at best, my father and his three friends set out on horseback to find this "wonderful valley," as the old monk called it. After weeks of searching, they found nothing that even remotely resembled the valley described to them. They were becoming discouraged and were about to return to where they left my mother and the others. It was early morning, and they were sitting around their campfire, discussing what they should do. Something caused my father to look into the shadows of the nearby forest. What he saw caused him to freeze. He could not move.

Something was standing just inside the shadows that made it difficult to make out. But when his eyes adjusted to the dim light, there was no mistaking what he saw. He told the others in a quiet voice to sit where they were and to do nothing. He rose slowly to his feet and raised his hands to show he meant no harm. The others did not know what was going on, but they did just as my father told them. After studying my father for several seconds, it stepped out from the shadows. My father is the first to admit when he saw the creature standing so close, in the full light of day, it was all he could do to keep his knees from buckling. Somehow, he was able to stay on his feet. The others had not seen the creature and were sitting quietly, just as they had been asked to do. My father knew exactly what the creature was."

"Come on, Dorje," Jeff blurted out unable to keep quiet any longer. "What the heck was the thing anyway?"

"Okay, I'm getting to that next. What was standing not far in front of him was the legendary creature of the Himalayas . . . a yeti. Or probably better known in the outside world as the abominable snowman. It was huge, close to nine feet tall, hairy all over its body, and standing upright just like we humans. It was a fearsome looking thing. There was something that struck my father right away. It was the look on the yeti's face. To this day, he still remembers. Never had he seen such a look of distress. Actually, it was because of this look that my father knew the creature meant them no harm. Call it intuition, whatever, but somehow he knew the yeti was asking for their help.

"Both stood facing each other for a long time. The yeti also must have sensed he was in no danger from my father.

"Very calmly, my father told his friends what to expect when they turned their heads. 'In no way,' he told them in a soft, firm voice, 'are you to show any fear or any sign of trying to harm the creature.' They did exactly as he had told them and soon they too felt at ease.

"Just before it turned to walk away, the yeti gave a sort of low, pitiful sound and actually made a motion with its arms as though he wanted them to follow it."

"What about their horses?" Jeff asked in a hushed tone. "Boy, I'll tell you, I really had a hard time getting Hercules to settle down. He must have really gotten a pretty strong whiff of the yeti."

"The horses were tethered a little distance away in some good grass. Also, the wind was blowing in the wrong direction for them to get any scent. Anyway, they realized something was very wrong, and the yeti was trying to tell them he needed their help. Quickly they made a decision. They would follow the yeti. They grabbed a few supplies and almost had to trot to keep up with the yeti's loping walk. They did not have the slightest idea where they were being led or how long it would take to get there. Every so often, the large creature would pause and turn around just to make sure they were still following. On and on they walked. There really was no trail, only a very faint track. The yeti began to climb up the side of a very high mountain. They followed. Higher and higher they were led until they were walking in a vast field of snow. The snow was firm, so it did not slow them down. Finally, the yeti stopped.

"When they got close enough, they could see it was standing on the edge of a narrow but deep crevasse in the snow. The yeti was looking to the crevasse and making a kind of low, soothing sound. It did this several times until there came a return call from deep inside the crevasse. That's when they noticed the footprints. They were not nearly as big as the yeti's who was standing beside them. These footprints looked like they might be from a young yeti, and they ended at the edge of the opening. They knew right away what had happened.

"The smaller yeti had somehow fallen into the icy depths of the crevasse and was trapped. They could see the marks it made at the very edge when it slipped. They had only one choice. One of them would have to go down and try to free the other yeti. They held a quick conference. The blacksmith, who was the smallest in the group, volunteered. They each had a good rope, so they tied them together. Tying one end around his chest, the blacksmith went over the side. The others acted as anchors and fed out the rope as he needed it. The big yeti stood close by, watching nervously, and began making several different sounds to the trapped yeti. He was probably telling it not to be afraid; help was on its way.

"Down deep into the depths climbed the blacksmith. Then, he was on the bottom. The snow was very soft. It took several minutes, but when his eyes adjusted to the dim light, he could see the other yeti sitting upright not far from where he stood. Slowly, he edged closer. He talked in a soothing voice, trying to make the yeti understand that he was there to help. It seemed to work. When he was close enough, the yeti stood as if to tell him it was not seriously injured. He untied the rope from around his chest and carefully tied it around the yeti. It did not move. Every once in a while, the yeti above the crevasse would make a sound like it was trying to reassure the other. When this would happen, the trapped yeti would answer. After making sure the rope was secure, the blacksmith called to the others to begin pulling the yeti up. The tightening of the rope startled the yeti, but the blacksmith was soon able to calm it down. Slowly, the yeti was lifted toward the thin sliver of light and freedom.

"After what seemed a very long time and a lot of hard work, they were able to finally pull the young, still frightened yeti out onto solid snow. The scene that followed may sound even stranger than what I have already told you. Quickly, the rope was untied. The young yeti sat in the snow, trying to adjust to being free. Suddenly, it jumped up and ran to the waiting arms of the adult. They hugged and made what must have been sounds of happiness. Each seemed to try to comfort the other, and there were tears in both their eyes. It was a very touching scene. It was easy to tell there was a great deal of love between the two. What their relationship was they could only guess, but they thought the larger yeti was probably the parent of the smaller one.

"The small group was so taken by what they had just seen that it took a yell from the blacksmith to remind them that it was time they pulled him out. This did not take long because he was a lot smaller and lighter than the yeti.

"For several minutes, my father and his friends stood together, each thankful they were able to be helpful. Standing there, my father began looking around. They had been intent on helping rescue the yeti and failed to see the spectacular scenery. Looking down, his eyes became fixed on something far below where they were standing. 'Could it be,' he said in wonderment.

"In his excitement, my father grabbed the blacksmith's arm so hard he let out a cry of pain. He quickly apologized, telling them all to look where he was pointing."

"What did he see," asked Jeff impatiently.

Dorje continued, "My father said to the others, 'Look at that. Look at where I am pointing.' Far below, they saw a valley, but this valley was different. They could tell it was quite big. What struck them most was that even from high up on the side of the mountain, the valley's lush green appearance, which was laced by the silver threads of many streams, looked like it might be the valley they had been searching for. Like the old monk had told them, it was surrounded on all sides by steep mountains. They could not see an entrance, but if this was the valley, they knew there was an entrance. However, finding it might be next to impossible. The old monk said it was so well hidden, it was only by sheer chance he stumbled onto it.

"The yetis had been standing quietly nearby. They seemed to sense by the humans' actions that they wanted to reach the valley. The yetis knew this valley so well because it was full of good things for them to eat. They began to slowly walk down the mountain. The larger yeti turned and made a motion for them to follow. Again, they did not know where they were being taken, but they thought probably back to their campsite. The farther they walked, the more it looked as though they were not going in the direction they came from. In fact, the direction they were going seemed to be taking them toward the valley. At times, the going was very steep and rugged. When they eventually reached the bottom, the ground was flat and the going much easier. The Yetis walked toward a smaller but even more jagged set of peaks. Would they have to cross these? They hoped not.

"They were walking several yards behind when the yetis made a sharp turn that took them behind some large boulders. When my father reached the spot, the Yetis had disappeared. They had simply vanished. The ground was too rocky to follow their footprints. All they could see was a huge jumble of debris. They knew there had to be some kind of opening or cave. They spread out and began to search. After they were looking for several minutes, someone—I think it was the blacksmith—gave a yell. When the others saw him, they could see he was pointing at something and was very excited. What he was pointing at was a well-concealed opening in the rock wall that led into some kind of passage.

"Now, I want to tell you, this was not the way we came into the valley. The way my father came in was what is used today as the emergency escape route. Hopefully, it will never be needed for that purpose. Still, it is used, but not very often. Even so, it's guarded just like the entrance we entered. Now, to get back to my story.

"They went through the opening and walked down the passage, which was really a slit in the rock wall and was probably created during the ice age. The light was very dim. When they reached the far end, the Yetis were waiting just outside. It took a while before their eyes adjusted to the brightness of the sun. When their eyes did adjust and they began to look around them, they knew the yetis had led them to the valley they were searching for . . . the valley the old monk had told them about. To them it looked even more beautiful than the monk said it was. They were so fascinated; they were unable to speak.

The first thing they did was to try to make the yetis understand how thankful they were for being shown how to get into the valley. Then they held a short meeting. They would camp where they were for the night. The next day they would go back to their original camp. My father and the blacksmith would then return to the valley with their horses and some supplies. The other two would return to where their people were waiting and lead them to the valley. This, they knew, would be very dangerous, because they had to avoid the Chinese at all costs. If the Chinese somehow got wind of their escape, they would send troops to stop them. Because of the number of people and amount of livestock and supplies, the move would have to be done in stages. If everything went okay, they estimated it would take three weeks to a month.

While they were gone, my father and the blacksmith would spend their time exploring as much of the valley as they could."

"I guess things must have gone according to plan," Jeff said. "The Chinese do not know about the valley."

"Yes," replied Dorje, "but they had several close calls. They did not even want other Tibetans to know where they were going. When asked, they said they were going to try to find better pasture for their animals and left it at that. They did not travel straight to the valley. Instead, they followed animal trails and trails that were rarely used. They tried to cover their tracks as much as possible. The job of the younger members was to walk behind the main party and wipe out as much of their trail as they could. They did this by using tree branches as brooms. It was very hard work. And it was certainly not an easy journey for anyone. I have gotten ahead of myself, Jeff."

Jeff was about to ask Dorje another question, but he thought, the heck with it, and waited to hear the rest of Dorje's thrilling tale.

"The yetis," continued Dorje, "disappeared at sundown but were back at sunup. My father offered to share some food with them, but they would not take any. He held out both hands with some tsampa in each, but the larger yeti patted his stomach as if to say they had eaten and were full. After breakfast, my father and his friends returned to where they had left the horses and supplies. The yetis went with them and acted as guides. It was late in the day when they reached the camp, so they decided to stay for the night. The next morning, before daylight, my father, the blacksmith, and the yetis were on their way back to the valley. Before you have a chance to ask," Dorje teased, "the horses really did make a fuss when they first saw and got a whiff of the yetis' scent. It was not too long, though, before they were able to quiet them down and get on the trail. When they returned to the valley, they camped in the same spot. There was a bubbling spring for fresh, cold water, and plenty of firewood and grass for the horses. It was very comfortable and would be their permanent camp. The next day, they would begin to explore the valley.

"They were finished eating breakfast by the time the sun's first bright rays began to edge their way over the distant peaks. The yetis showed up just as they were saddling the horses. The first thing they wanted to look for was a suitable site where they could begin building their permanent village when the others arrived. It was early in the afternoon when they found the right spot, which is where the village is now located. It really surprised them because it had everything they were looking for; several springs of fresh water, lots of rich grass, good soil to grow vegetables, and plenty of trees and rocks they could use for building materials.

"Each day, they would ride out into the valley to explore. They checked out the soil to see where the best area was to plant their crops and fruit orchards, and they looked for pastures for their animals. The valley was already home to several herds of wild yak and deer. They found several ponds, which dotted the floor of the valley and were home to large numbers of ducks and geese. They found all kinds of wildlife that made the valley their home. Most of the birds and animals they saw were very tame—probably because they had never seen a human.

"One day, while exploring the far side of the valley, the older yeti signaled for them to follow. What he wanted them to see was the other entrance into the valley, the one we used.

"Their days were busy and passed very quickly. The more they explored, the more they came to realize this was not just a beautiful, fertile valley, but a paradise for all the creatures who lived in it. They knew it was going to be a paradise not only for themselves, but for the rest of their people, too.

There were a few times when my father and the blacksmith had to camp temporarily in other parts of the valley. It was after one of those times when they had just returned to their main camp after spending a few days in a distant part of the valley. It was nearing dark. They were both very tired and had just settled themselves around the campfire. They were sitting and relaxing when they heard the sound of horses' hooves echoing from inside the passageway. They tensed. The yetis, who had been sitting several feet away, must have sensed there might be danger. They moved closer to the fire so they would be near my father and the blacksmith, ready to protect them. The sound grew louder. Whoever it was getting closer to the exit of the passage. Suddenly, the sound stopped."

chapter 14

At that point in the story, they were called to the evening meal. It looked as though Jeff would have to wait until after they finished eating before Dorje would be able to continue his tale. He only hoped he could wait that long.

While they were eating, Dorje told Jeff the helicopter would be coming the next day, and the letter he wrote would be given to the pilot to mail. That took a load off Jeff's mind. He knew Trudy would get the letter in about a week. She would be brought up to date about what had happened since he left on his adventure.

After eating, Dorje could tell that Jeff was anxious for him to continue his story. Dorje took him by the arm. He guided Jeff back to the same room they had been in before dinner and sat him down.

"Now, where was I?"

"You left off where the sounds of the horses' hooves stopped," came Jeff's quick reply.

"Oh, yes, now I remember. They were all ready for whatever was about to happen. As they crouched, straining to hear, the noise began again. The horse was moving, coming closer and closer.

When they knew it was about to come out of the passageway, my father whispered, 'get ready.' It was a very tense moment.

"As the horse and rider came out into the open, they were just about to jump him. However, at the very last second, they saw who it was. To their great relief and joy, it was one of the two men who were sent to bring the others there to the valley. At that exact moment, his horse either saw or got the yeti's scent. The horse began to buck something fierce. It was only the rider's skill that saved him from being bucked off and possibly injured. After the horse finally quieted down, they had a warm reunion.

"As they sat around the campfire, drinking yak-butter tea, he told them he had ridden ahead to tell my father the rest of the party would probably make it to the valley sometime early the next afternoon. He told them about how three different times they had to avoid Chinese patrols. Once, they were very nearly caught. They were very fortunate because there was a large forested area where they were able to ride until the danger had passed. With so many people and animals and supplies, he really did not know how they were able to do it, but they did. That last encounter was about two weeks ago. These last two weeks, the country they traveled through became so wild and remote they did not see anything but a few wild yaks. They sat talking until late that night. The yetis, like always, had left at sundown. They did not return the next morning. My father said he felt the yetis knew they had helped them as much as they could, and it was time for them to carry on by themselves."

"Has anyone ever seen one since that time? Do they ever visit the valley?" Jeff questioned.

"On rare occasions one will be spotted. There is a small side valley, which is where the springs are that form the headwaters of the stream where you caught the big trout. We know they frequent this spot. Why? We don't know. There is a large, flat rock next to the springs. Several times a year, the people here in the village take dried fruit and place it on the rock. The people know the yetis watch over them, and this is their way of thanking them."

"How do you know they watch over the people?"

"I will give you an example of the most recent thing that happened. It was on my last visit here, and it was almost time for me to leave. First, I wanted to say goodbye to a young friend of mine. At that time, he was ten years old. He is very bright and when he is ready, I am sure he will be sent outside to further his education. I rode over to his house to see him. When I arrived, both his father and mother were outside. I could tell by the expression on their faces something was wrong. His father, who was saddling his horse, told me the boy's horse had just come home but without his son. He said the boy had ridden out to check on some of their sheep. The sheep he went to check on were grazing not far from the entrance to the small side valley I told you about earlier. I rode out with the father to try to find the boy. It is probably about a four-mile ride, so we took off at a fast gallop. We had gone perhaps halfway when we saw him coming toward us in the distance. When he saw us, he began to run. When we reached him, we were really glad he was not hurt in any way. However, he did have a story to tell us."

"Now come on, don't beat around the bush, Dorje. Tell me, what was his story?"

"Okay, just calm down and I'll tell you," Dorje said. "It seems when the boy got out to the sheep he was to check on, he heard the sound of an ewe that could mean only one thing . . . she had either become lost or had separated from her lamb. He dismounted and walked through some thick, tall bushes to reach where the sound came from. He saw her when he reached the other side. She was standing next to the edge of a large rockslide. He could hear the bleating of the lamb coming from somewhere in the jumble of rocks. After a short search, he found the lamb. It had somehow wedged itself between two boulders. It was trapped and could not move. It did not take long before he was able to move enough rock so he could free the little fellow. When he carried it back and placed it next to its mother, they both took off through the bushes to join the other sheep. They were grazing peacefully in the tall meadow grass.

"Just after the ewe and its lamb had run back to the other sheep, for some unknown reason, he felt he was in danger. Slowly he turned his head. What he saw caused the hair on the back of his neck to stand up. On top of a boulder not more than twenty feet away, in a crouched position and ready to spring, was a large snow leopard. The leopard snarled menacingly, showing its long, white fangs. Now, let me tell you, normally these animals stay high among the peaks. This one must have strayed into the valley and was probably stalking the ewe when the boy arrived on the scene. It was mad because it had just been cheated out of an easy meal.

"Now, all of its attention was focused on the boy. What the boy did next probably saved his life. He gave a loud, blood-curdling yell that caught the leopard off guard. IT caused the leopard to delay its leap just long enough for the boy to climb a tree standing a few feet away. It was a tall tree, but the trunk was very slender and would certainly not have supported anyone who weighed more than him. He climbed as high as he could until, because of his weight, the trunk began to bend. The leopard, in its anger, made a long leap off the boulder and tried to climb the tree. Because the trunk was so slender, the leopard could not get a good grip with its claws and kept falling back to the ground. This made him even angrier. Each time it would try to climb the tree, the tree would begin to sway. Believe me, my frightened young friend said he held on for all he was worth. The leopard, finally realizing it could not get at his prey, decided to lie on the ground and wait. It became a standoff to see who could out wait whom. During this time, the boy's horse must have gotten wind of the leopard, panicked, and ran for home. He does not really remember how long he was in the tree when he heard a crashing in the bushes. Out burst this huge, hairy creature, and it headed straight toward the leopard. I remember the big smile on his face when he told us about the leopard jumping to its feet. It was so scared, it ran straight up the side of the mountain. He really laughed when he said he had never seen anything move so fast. After the leopard ran off, the creature motioned for the boy to climb down from the tree. Then it walked off into the bushes. Of course, what the boy saw was a yeti, and he knew this. Everyone in the valley knows about them."

"That's really some story. So, what you're telling me is the yetis are kind of the guardians for the people here in the valley?"

"Well, yes. I guess that is what they are. No one knows how many yetis there are, but believe me, the people in the valley are very glad to know they are watching over them."

"I can't say I blame them. Concerning the footprint I saw, I guess I really didn't have anything to worry about after all."

"No, but of course, at the time you did not know that. Actually, the yeti was probably just checking you out."

chapter 15

Jeff spent the next several days fishing, riding Hercules, and taking some hikes. One morning he was out behind the blacksmith's shop, brushing Hercules, when he heard his name being called. When he looked to see who it was, he saw the blacksmith hurrying toward him.

"Word has just arrived that Colonel Chin and his men have left the monastery. They will be gone for several weeks, and he only left a few men and Captain Ling behind. This is better than we hoped. We thought for sure he would leave at least a dozen men behind."

Jeff hurried back to Dorje's house, where Dorje was waiting for him.

"Yes," he answered Jeff, "Colonel Chin has left the monastery. The runner said only two soldiers and Captain Ling were left to guard your parents. The runner that brought the news is going to be our guide. A meeting has been called for this evening. It won't be long now," Dorje said as he slapped Jeff on the shoulder.

The meeting did not last long. Dorje's father and the others attending decided because only two soldiers were at the monastery, only Dorje, Jeff, and the runner would be in the rescue party. They decided the fewer, the better.

"They have to get in and out as fast as possible," stated Dorje's father firmly. "If everything goes like we hope," he continued, "they won't even know his parents are gone until the next morning."

That evening, the runner, whose name was Bajay, showed Jeff and Dorje the map of the inside of the monastery he had brought with him. Compared to many, it was not a large monastery. Yet it was a jumble of rooms of all sizes, and hallways where, unless you knew your way, it would be very easy to get lost. An X marked the spot of each room where Jeff's parents slept. He could certainly understand why they needed a guide to get to them. One good thing was that it did look like their rooms were not far apart. When Jeff asked Bajay if he would have any trouble finding the rooms, he replied that he knew the inside of the monastery like it was his own house. He added that the person who would let them in had to get right back to his room. This would give him a much better chance of not being discovered as the one who unlocked the door.

"Hopefully," Bajay said, "when they find out I am missing, they will put all the blame on me. Since I am not returning to the monastery to work, it does not matter. My job there will be done, and I will come back to my home here in the valley, but I will not return with you. I will return on foot by another way."

Because they were leaving several hours before daylight the next morning, they knew they had to get at least a few hours of sleep. Before they retired, Dorje's father told them everything would be ready when it was time for them to leave. Jeff was very pleased when he was told he would be riding Hercules. Due to Bajay not returning with them, he would ride on one of the two horses Jeff's parents would be riding after they were rescued.

So finally, it was time for bed and hopefully sleep—easier said than done. Jeff was so keyed up that he could not sleep. He wondered if Dorje was having the same problem.

They were up and had something to eat. To his surprise, Jeff felt well rested and ready to go. While eating, Jeff asked Bajay how the contact inside the monastery would know to let them in.

"At midnight, beginning tonight, he will be at the main entrance to let us in. If we have not shown up after five nights, he is to assume the plans to free your parents have been changed."

"Have you seen my parents?" Jeff asked rather hesitantly.

"No. I am not allowed to see or talk to them. I do know they are in good health."

This last statement helped to ease the tension building inside him, and he was able to relax at last.

When they were almost ready to leave, Dorje handed Jeff a small sword and a knife. "Put these in your belt," he told him. When Jeff did, Dorje looked at him and with deep feeling in his voice said, "My friend, now you look like a real Khamban." This statement caused a surge of pride to swell within Jeff's body.

They had been underway for many hours before the first rays of the sun crept over the rugged crags of the most distant ridge. Jeff knew they were in for a long, tough day in the saddle. He was glad he had been riding almost every day and felt he would have no problems. He knew Dorje did not want to try and free Jeff's parents that night. Instead, he wanted to rest not only themselves but the horses also. The attempt to free them would be carried out the next night. Even though he was anxious and hated for his parents to have to spend another night in that place, he knew this was a sound plan. They certainly would need to be as fresh as possible.

Not long after leaving the valley, they began to climb steadily. The narrow, rock-strewn trail was steep; as steep as any trail Jeff had ever ridden. Often the trail would be so steep they would have to get off their horses and walk. When they did, what they would do was get behind their horse, take hold of its tail, and just let the horse pull them along. The horses did not seem to mind this at all. In fact, they acted as though it was just part of their job. Much of this was new to Hercules, but he took it in stride. Eventually, the trail became so steep and narrow; Dorje said they would have to walk the rest of the way to the pass.

It was in the early afternoon, when they climbed the last steep pitch to the top, that Dorje promised they would have something to eat. There was no shade. The sun beat down on them the same as if they were in the middle of the Sahara Desert. Instead of sand, they were surrounded by a huge field of snow. They were well above the tree line. How high they were, Jeff could only guess, but he actually felt as though he was sitting at the very top of the world. It was not an unpleasant feeling. They paused only long enough to eat some dried yak meat and a hard boiled egg. While they were eating, Jeff was thinking to himself, who would have believed only a few short months ago that today he would be sitting atop one of the loneliest, most remote places in the world? He kept reminding himself he should feel lonely, when actually he felt anything but lonely. In that short time, his eyes were never still. There was too much to see. The mountains off to the right were cloaked from top to bottom with the deep green of thick pine forests, which was a real study in contrast to the bare, rocky, snow-covered peak where they were sitting. Off slightly to their left and many thousands of feet below, Jeff could see the thin line of a pewter colored river cutting its way through the meadows and forests of a distant valley.

"Even from this height, that looks like a pretty nice valley," he said, showing them where he was looking.

"It is," replied Dorje, "it is. In fact, that is the exact valley where the monastery is located. From here, it is hidden from our view because it sits on the far side of the low hill you can see there, near the upper end of the valley."

"So that's the place I've come so far to get to," said Jeff in a low, serious voice.

"Yes, that is the place," replied Dorje just as seriously. "As you can see, even from where we are, there is much thick forest, so we will have good cover. It will take several hours before we even get close to the valley. If we really push it, we should be there before dark."

As though programmed, the three of them stood at exactly the same time. Before them lay the danger involved in the long, hard descent down the mountain. Once they reached the valley, they would be faced with another kind of danger—a danger more terrible than Jeff might ever have imagined. The kind of danger only a madman can create. He might be forced to make split second decisions—decisions that might make the difference between success or failure. Jeff knew if he was faced with such a choice and he made the wrong one . . . well, he shuddered at the thought of what the consequences might be. Was he up to it? Was he even capable in the first place? Could Dorje and Bajay rely on him if a crisis should occur? Would he be able to carry his weight? He knew Dorje was counting on him. All of these questions, and more, kept flashing through his brain.

Dorje said it was too steep to ride, so they would have to lead the horses down much of the way. Just before they started, Jeff faced Dorje and said, "No matter what might happen, no matter what we might come up against, I will not let you down."

"I know that," was Dorje's simple but meaningful reply.

Down they went. At times, the trail was so steep they could not keep their footing. They would just slide until they stopped. The horses seemed to have a unique way of getting down the steep parts. When they came to one, they would drop back onto their haunches and slide forward, using their front legs as brakes. They were really good at it, and it always worked. Not once did a horse lose control. They seemed to be almost as sure-footed as a mountain goat.

It was well into the afternoon when they finally reached level ground. The trail began to get wider as it twisted its way through the dense pine forest. Because of the thick carpet of pine needles, the sound of the horses' hooves was nothing more than a soft whisper when compared to the hard thudding noise they made when walking on harder ground.

Bajay, who was in the lead, stopped and told them to stay very close. They were about to leave the trail and cut through the thick trees. He did not want anyone to become separated. The distant sound of the river soon became a loud, angry roar. At that point, Bajay left the trail and headed into the shadow of the deep woods. The pleasant smell of pine was everywhere. Jeff, who was in the rear, leading the extra horse, made a special effort to stay close. The last thing he wanted was to become separated and get lost. It was nearly twilight, the time of day when there is neither sunlight nor darkness, when Bajay called a halt. They had reached the place where they would cross the river. To Jeff's relief, the river, at this point, was nothing like its roaring, wild self farther upstream. So swift, it could easily sweep even the strongest horse off its feet. Here, it flowed smooth and placid.

Once they were across the icy waters, Bajay led them downstream, still keeping to the trees as the river made a large horseshoe bend. At the bottom of the bend, Bajay steered them into a small grass-covered clearing and told them to dismount and tie their horses. Once the horses were tied, Bajay told them to follow him. He stopped at the edge of the trees but was careful to keep behind a heavy growth of bushes, just in case.

"There," said Bajay, "is the monastery where your parents are being held prisoner."

The monastery sat at the bottom of the low hill. There were three levels to the building. The first floor was where the multipurpose rooms and chapel were located. The second and third floors contained most of the small cell-like rooms where the monks once lived. The building itself was whitewashed with beams and supports made of wood. These were painted in blue, yellow, and red. Actually, it was a very remarkable looking structure.

"That's a pretty big building," stated Jeff. "If this is considered a rather small monastery, I can't even imagine the size of one of the larger monasteries. There must be more than a hundred and fifty rooms in this place."

"I do not know how many rooms are in the monastery," came Bajay's reply, "but Colonel Chin does not use them all. Many are left abandoned. Many monasteries are built high on a cliff for protection against bandits and invaders. As you can see, this one was not. Its protection was because the valley is so remote and like our valley, a secret place."

"A secret place, that is, until Colonel Chin somehow discovered it," broke in Dorje.

"Yes, and how sad it is," answered Bajay, "not only because he has forced the monks to leave and made the monastery his own special headquarters, but for what he has done to the priceless works of sacred art, the library, and the holy objects that were in the monastery. Many of them have been housed there since it was first built. They were irreplaceable. Colonel Chin has destroyed almost everything."

"That is really terrible," sympathized Jeff, "but tell me, "when was it built? It sure does look old."

"It is," replied Bajay, "and it was built in about the middle of the twelfth century."

"Wow," came Jeff's low response. "It's hard for me to believe that something like that is still standing after all of those years, especially way off in a place like this."

As the three of them stood looking at the monastery, Bajay told Jeff to look where he was pointing. "That is the part of the monastery where your parents are being held. I know it's getting dark, but look really hard. Do you see that small window on the second tier? Not one of the larger ones, but that small one."

"Yes, I see it. I see where you mean."

That statement caused a sudden quiver to come to Jeff's lips, but he was able to fight off the tears. He asked where the room was that his father slept in.

"His room is just across and down a narrow hallway. He also has a small window, but it faces in the other direction, so we cannot see it."

It was Dorje who cocked his head as if he had heard something.

"There it is again," he said. "Do you hear it?"

They did. It was getting closer . . . close enough now so they could identify the sound. It was the unmistakable clack, clack, clacking noise of a helicopter when in flight. Even though they were well hidden, they did not move.

The helicopter came in low over the trees from down the valley. They did not see it until it was just about to land behind some trees off to one side of the monastery.

"I do not understand this," stated Bajay. "Colonel Chin was supposed to have gone in the helicopter when his troops left. Why has it come back? Something must be up. There may have been a change in their plans. Perhaps the soldiers are on their way back. If that is so, we could be in real trouble. There is no way we can get Jeff's parents out if they return. There are just too many of them. They would hunt us down. There's just no way we could escape, especially since they have the helicopter. With only three of us, it would be hopeless."

"What should we do? I can't let my parents stay a prisoner of that mad man. I have come this far, and I'm not going to leave without them."

"Okay," answered Dorje, "let me think a minute. Now, we

don't know for sure if Colonel Chin was in the helicopter, and we don't know if his troops are on their way back. They only left several days ago, so it seems a bit unlikely they would be returning so soon. Yet there might have been some kind of mess up or something. The only way to find out is for Bajay to go to the monastery tonight at midnight and talk to the person who is going to let us in. Hopefully they will know just what is going on. Bajay, how does that sound to you?"

"That seems to be the only thing we can do," Bajay answered firmly.

"We may have a change in plans," added Dorje. "It all depends on what you find out. No matter if the situation has changed or not, tell the person inside to wait one hour after you leave. We may want to get in tonight. If we don't show up in an hour, he is to come back at midnight tomorrow night."

The time seemed to pass very quickly. They had some more dried yak meat and a hard-boiled egg for the evening meal and then took it easy until it was time for Bajay to go to the monastery. Before he left, he told them if he wasn't back within an hour, they were to assume something had gone wrong.

While he was gone, Jeff asked Dorje about Bajay. "He was born in the valley like me," he began, "was sent to school in India, and returned to the valley not long before my father was informed about your parents being held by Colonel Chin. My father needed someone else to work inside the monastery. When my father asked Bajay, he willingly volunteered. He was smuggled into the valley and was given a job in the monastery as a janitor. Colonel Chin really likes things to be kept clean and shiny. This was the perfect job because it gave Bajay a lot of freedom to get to know the inside of the monastery. As he said, once we have freed your parents, his job at the monastery will be done. What he would like to do next is become a teacher in our school."

The hour was nearly up, and they were getting worried. Had

something happened? They soon realized they had worried for nothing when they saw Bajay coming toward them.

When he was close enough, Dorje asked if he had been able to find out anything.

"Yes," came his reply.

"Well, don't keep us in suspense," Dorje said before Bajay could continue.

"Colonel Chin was in the helicopter, and he is really angry. I guess he is so angry he locked himself in his quarters with strict instructions he was not, under any circumstances, to be disturbed."

"Why was he so angry?"

"It seems the maneuvers he and his soldiers were supposed to take part in were canceled at the last minute by one of the big Chinese generals."

"Uh-oh," exclaimed Dorje. "Did you find out when the troops are supposed to get back here to the monastery?"

"Yes. They should be back within a day, two at the most. It depends on how hard they are pushed."

"How was our friend in the monastery able to get all of this information?" Dorje asked.

"The helicopter pilot told him. And after they landed, Colonel Chin told the pilot to refuel the helicopter because they would be taking off early the next morning."

"Did he say where they would be going?"

"No. He just told him to refuel and to be ready for an early morning takeoff."

"Well, that settles it," declared Dorje. "Is there somewhere we can hide in the monastery that's close to the rooms where Jeff's parents are being held?"

"Yes. There is a storeroom almost directly across the hall from where his mother is kept. I don't think the guards ever check it out."

"Great. Now where does the helicopter pilot sleep?"

"He sleeps clear at the other end of the monastery. His room is close to Colonel Chin's quarters. Captain Ling's room is right next to the pilot's room. You see, the small cell-like rooms where Jeff's parents are kept are in the part of the building where most of the monks used to sleep. Now the soldiers use them. The only people sleeping in that part right now are the two soldiers who were left behind to guard Jeff's parents. From what I was just told, they have not been taking their guard duties very seriously."

"Do you think we can get to that store room tonight without being seen? Do you know where we can get some rope?"

"Yes. I think we can. The guard will probably be asleep at his post, which is a chair in an alcove at the far end of the hall. As for rope, you are in luck. There are several coils of it in the storeroom. I take it you have some kind of plan."

"Yes," answered Dorje, "but for it to work, we have to get inside the monastery tonight. Once we are in the storeroom, I'll tell you both what I have come up with."

"We still have plenty of time to get to the front entrance before our friend leaves for the night, but we had better get going," stated Bajay.

Jeff had been listening intently to what his two friends had been saying. He was anxious to get going and told them so.

In a single file, with Bajay leading, they left the cover of the bushes. The thick, knee-high grass was wet with dew. Jeff could feel its cool wetness through his clothing. Soon they passed through the thin line of high bushes in front of the monastery. On the other side and off to their left sat Colonel Chin's helicopter. Dorje whispered for them to stop and wait while he checked it out. It did not take long. When he was finished, by the look on his face, Dorje seemed very pleased with what he saw.

Bajay led them through an open gate into a large, rock-paved courtyard. He cautioned them to be very quiet and keep close to him in the deep shadows.

The huge, thick, double wooden doors at the entrance of the monastery were painted a bright red. Bajay gave three firm raps on the door with the handle of his knife. They could hear the heavy cross bar being lifted, and one of the doors was opened just enough so they could squeeze through. They were inside. The door was shut and the bar replaced. While the three of them held a whispered discussion, Jeff let his eyes wander around the interior of the large room. There was not much to see except for some large clay urns sitting along one of the walls; otherwise, the room was empty.

When the whispered discussion was over, the one who let them in left rather quickly. He had done his part, and now they were on their own. Bajay tapped Jeff on the shoulder and motioned for him to stay between Dorje and himself.

Bajay led them into an even larger room where there were several lines of long, wooden tables, each side lined with benches. This had been the monasteries main dining room. Next, they were led through a series of narrow, twisting, maze-like passages and smaller rooms.

"What a place," Jeff thought to himself. "I'm sure glad we didn't have to follow that map because we would have almost certainly gotten lost." He wondered how long it took Bajay to learn how to find his way around.

Eventually, they came to a long, straight, narrow hall that was lined on each side with wood doors. These were the rooms where the monks had slept, and two of these rooms were where his parents were sleeping. Bajay told them to stay where they were while he went to check on the guard. He returned shortly and told them he was sleeping in his chair. They should have no trouble getting to the storeroom.

As they tiptoed down the hall, Jeff could actually feel the closeness of his parents. It gave him goose bumps. Halfway down the hall, Bajay gave the signal to be extra careful. They were about to pass the open door of the room where the other guard slept. They really did have to watch their step because the rock floor was very slick and uneven. Jeff glanced in when they passed the room and saw a figure lying on a cot. By the sound of his snoring, they knew he must be asleep. A little farther down the hall, Bajay stopped and carefully opened a door. The storeroom was a good size, and on the floor was a jumble of clay pots, boxes, coils of rope, and spider webs . . . lots of spider webs. Along with snakes, Jeff hated spiders but realized there was not a thing he could do about it. He was thankful the room was not full of snakes, as well.

"Do you think we can talk in here without being heard, just in case the guard wakes up?"

"I think so," replied Bajay, "but to be on the safe side, let's go to the rear of the room to talk."

"Jeff," Dorje began, "I know you want to get to your parents just as soon as you can, especially since we are so close. I don't blame you, but I am afraid we will have to wait until about an hour before it gets light before we can do that. The reason for waiting is if the guard should check on them and they are not there, he would certainly give the alarm. Maybe Colonel Chin himself might have a reason to come to see them. You just never know. For my plan to work, we have to wait."

"What is your plan?" Jeff asked, trying to hide his disappointment.

"I'm coming to that. Bajay, is there a window close by that is large enough for us to escape through?"

Bajay thought for several seconds and then answered. "Yes, there is a window. I think it would be perfect. It is in the big room at the end of the hall. There is even a thick pillar where we could tie the rope."

"Great! Now what about the guard? Bajay, you will have to tie and gag not only the guard on duty, but also the one sleeping in his room. It is very important that you let the guard on duty see and recognize you."

"Why?" Bajay questioned.

"So you will be the one blamed for freeing Jeff's parents."

"Good idea," Bajay said, chuckling. "I'm not coming back here, anyway."

"What about the helicopter? It will certainly be able to find us," stated Jeff.

"That comes next. Jeff, do you remember at the meeting where my father happened to mention I had been well trained?"

"Yes, I do."

"Well, part of that training was to learn to fly a helicopter."

"You're kidding. That is fantastic," Jeff said excitedly. "Now I understand why we have to wait until nearly daylight to get out of here. But," he added, "can you fly a Chinese helicopter?"

"You saw me give it a quick check on our way in. Most of the Chinese army's helicopters were made in Russia. This one, however, as I suspected, was not. This particular helicopter is designed for flying at high altitudes. It was made in France and was originally designed to do search and rescue work in the European Alps. I knew the Chinese had a few, and how Colonel Chin got this one I will never know. Still, I am sure glad he did. It just so happens that the Indian army, where I learned to fly, also has a few of these same models that beside the pilot can carry three passengers. They are called Lamas. I spent a lot of hours learning to fly one of them. The helicopter that used to fly to the secret landing spot near our village is a Lama, only it is a larger model."

"What about Bajay? If the helicopter is able to carry only three passengers, how is he going to get back?"

"Have you forgotten? We have four horses tied in the woods. Since we won't be riding them in our escape, Bajay is going to take them back. Perhaps, Colonel Chin will think Bajay was the only one who helped your parents escape. He might think your father was able to fly the helicopter and Bajay left with them. If that part of the plan works, they won't go looking for him."

"We know the gas tanks were filled last night, but just how far can one of these things fly? Will we have enough gas?" Jeff asked hesitantly.

"More than enough," Dorje answered reassuringly. "One of 'these things,' as you put it, can fly a lot farther than we will be going when fully gassed. It is not gas that may be the problem; it is the weather. It can change in a matter of minutes. Fog, mist, clouds—these are what we have to be most concerned about. The route we will be flying takes us through a very narrow canyon. That is the most dangerous part of the trip. But we will make it. Please don't worry."

The last part of what Dorje said made Jeff feel more at ease, and he told him so.

"Well then, it's settled," said Dorje. "Now I want to check out the rope. In the meantime, you two had better try and get some rest. We have about an hour before we begin."

Both Jeff and Bajay sat on the floor with their backs to the wall. Even though it felt like a thousand butterflies were playing tag in his stomach, Jeff was able to doze off.

It seemed like he had just closed his eyes when Jeff felt Dorje's hand gently shake him. In a flash, he was wide awake and noticed Bajay was, also.

"Bajay, you know what you have to do. Don't forget, you have got to let at least the guard on duty see who you are. That is very important. I don't want Colonel Chin to think anyone from the outside knew anything about this place. Do you think you can take care of both of them by yourself? I have cut several lengths of rope to tie them with, and here are two long pieces of cloth you can use for gags. Again, I'm asking you, do you think you can do this?"

"I am a Khamban," he replied as he tapped his finger on the handle of his sword.

"Good for you," answered Dorje, patting Bajay on the shoulder. "After you have done your job, we will free Jeff's parents. If everything goes according to plan, we should be out of here in about thirty minutes."

Even though Jeff and Dorje both knew Bajay would do his job, they waited nervously. He was back in a surprisingly short amount of time, wearing a king sized grin on his face. He motioned for them to come out into the hall.

Because Jeff's father's room was closest to the window they were going to use to get out of the monastery, they thought it would be best to free his mother first.

When Bajay stopped in front of a door and told Jeff it was the door to his mother's room, his knees almost buckled, and he leaned against the wall for support.

Gathering strength, he whispered, "I want to remove the crossbar and open the door myself."

They stood back to give him plenty of room. He had a little trouble trying to get the bar free and waved Bajay away when he tried to help. A loud creaking noise went echoing down the hall when he opened the door. While Jeff went in, Dorje and Bajay stayed in the hall to keep a watch just in case. Jeff knew without being told that he must hurry.

Quickly and quietly, he moved to the side of the cot where his mother lay sleeping. For just a second, he hesitated, and then ever so gently touched her on the shoulder. Her eyes fluttered. He touched her a second time and whispered, "Mother, wake up. It's me, Jeff. I have come to take you home."

Her eyes opened and stared at him with a puzzled look of disbelief. "Jeff," she said haltingly. "Jeff, is that really you or am I dreaming again?"

"No, Mother, you are not dreaming. It's really me, honest," he answered. He gave her a slight pinch on the arm as proof.

"I knew you would come for us. Don't ask me how I knew,

but I knew," she said. She choked back tears as she gave him a warm hug.

"We haven't much time. You've got to get dressed. My friends are waiting in the hall, and we still have to get Dad."

She was up and dressed in a matter of seconds. Jeff quickly introduced her, and then Bajay led the way to a door on the other side of the hall.

The rooms were exactly the same. His father lay on his side, facing away from him. Jeff knew from past experience he would not wake as easily as his mother. His father was a very sound sleeper. It took a lot of shaking before he began to stir. His eyes finally opened, and it looked like he might start to struggle, but he was able to calm him down when he recognized who Jeff was. He also said he felt Jeff would somehow come for them. They also had a warm reunion.

"Dad, get up and get dressed," he urged. "Mom and my friends are waiting in the hall, and we have got to get out of here, now!"

That's all it took. He was up and dressed so fast, Jeff could hardly believe it.

After they were introduced, they followed Bajay through a curtained doorway at the end of the hall. The room they entered was large. On the outside wall was a good-sized shuttered window. Carefully, Bajay opened the shutters and peered out. Not far away, he could see the dark, skeletal-like outline of the helicopter. He was just about to say something when he jerked his head back inside. Something near the helicopter had moved. He motioned for the others to keep still. There it was again. There was no mistake. Someone was down there. Bajay watched as the shadow-like figure got in the helicopter and sat in the pilot's seat.

"Quick," Bajay demanded, "give me some rope and some rags. The pilot is checking out the helicopter. That means Colonel Chin probably wants to take off just as soon as it's light, and that isn't very long from now. I'm going down there and take care of the pilot. I think I had better blindfold him as well as tie and gag him just to play it safe. We don't want him to get a look at you or Jeff. When it is all clear, I'll give you a signal. You've got to get out and to the helicopter as fast as you can. I don't know how soon Colonel Chin will be coming, but it might be any minute now. After I give you the signal, I'm heading for the horses so I can get back on the trail. Dorje, give me some rope and rags. Jeff, tie the end of this long rope around the pillar nearest to the window."

They all wished Bajay good luck as he went over the edge of the window. They knew their escape was in his hands.

As Bajay dropped lightly to the ground, Jeff remembered the words Bajay said earlier: "I am a Khamban."

As silent as a ghost, Bajay crept across the open space between the monastery and the helicopter. Once, he froze instantly in his tracks when the pilot turned on the cabin light. He inched closer, waiting for his chance. When the pilot's foot touched the step as he left the cabin, Bajay knew it was now or never.

It was over in seconds. The pilot lay in an unconscious heap on the ground. After dragging him into some nearby bushes, he tied his hands and feet, put a gag in his mouth, and tied a blindfold over his eyes. When he was through, Bajay hurried to where Dorje could see him. He gave the all clear signal, turned, and vanished into the remaining darkness.

chapter 16

Dorje was first to go down the rope. Jeff's mother was next. He asked her if she thought she could make it without any trouble.

"Why of course," she answered firmly as she slipped over the side. She was soon standing by Dorje. Soon they were all safely on the ground.

"We have to get into the helicopter and off the ground as quickly as we can," Dorje said. "It will be light soon, and Colonel Chin might show up at any minute."

Inside the monastery, Colonel Chin and Captain Ling had just finished eating breakfast and were on their way out to the helicopter. They had just reached the front entrance when they heard the sound.

"Ah, Captain Ling," Colonel Chin said with a smug smile. "The pilot is starting the helicopter. He must have sensed we were on our way."

They walked faster. Just as they reached the edge of the courtyard, they stopped dead in their tracks. The helicopter was taking off without them.

"What is he doing?" Colonel Chin stammered. "How dare he do this."

They began to shout and shake their fists. Colonel Chin's face was turning purple with rage. He turned on Captain Ling, yelling and screeching. He asked why the pilot had left them. How dare he; did he know who he was dealing with? He was Colonel Chin, and someday he was going to rule the world! The mad colonel was actually frothing at the mouth. That's when Captain Ling stumbled on the pilot. He lay bound and gagged in the bushes.

The receding shadows of the night kept pace with the helicopter as it gained altitude. They were surrounded as far as they could see by a huge jumble of snow-covered peaks. They were well above the floor of the valley and still climbing, always climbing. Looking behind, Jeff could see the valley disappearing over a rock-covered ridge. Ahead, there was no sign of a trail or village. In fact, there was no sign of any kind of life, human or otherwise—only those jagged, ominous peaks.

For a long time, the atmosphere inside the helicopter was so tense, no one dared to speak. Finally, Dorje spoke.

"Mr. and Mrs. Thornton, I want to tell you just how happy I am to finally meet you. Jeff has told me a lot about you since he and I first met. I know the three of you have many things to talk about, but please wait. You will have plenty of time once we reach our destination."

"How long do you think it will take us," Jeff asked.

"That really depends on the weather. If it stays clear like it is now, we should be there in only a few hours. If we run into any kind of bad weather, we may have to find a place to land and wait for it to clear. You'll see soon enough, but we are going to be flying in tight quarters. First we have to fly over a pass."

"How high is the pass?"

"Well, I'll put it this way. I don't know exactly how high it is, but it isn't so high that we can't fly over it. That's not what I'm worried about. Once we are over the pass, we have to fly most of the remaining trip through a canyon. In some places, this canyon gets pretty narrow and makes a number of sharp curves. That's why I'm so concerned about the weather. We might not have enough room to turn back if we get caught in one of those narrow parts. I would like to fly over the canyon, but even this helicopter won't climb high enough to get over the peaks we'd have to fly over. So the canyon is the only way."

"Have you ever flown through the canyon before?"

"Only once, Jeff, and I was a passenger. That was a few years ago, but for some reason, I still remember like it was yesterday. Anyway, don't worry. I really do know how to fly one of these things. We will make it. What I would like is for each of you to really keep your eyes open and not to talk. That is unless you see something that I should know about. I really have to concentrate on my flying."

"Just one more thing. What should we be looking for?"

"Anything unusual: clouds closing in on us, fog, or anything that might prove to be dangerous. The more eyes the better. Like I said, I really have to concentrate on flying."

All through Jeff and Dorje's conversation, Jeff's parents sat quietly and close together with looks of disbelief on their faces. It was as though the fact they were free from Colonel Chin's grasp had not yet set into their minds.

They had been flying smoothly for some time when Dorje said, "Jeff, see that ridge ahead?"

"Yes!"

"And do you see the split in the ridge, like a big gun sight? We have to fly through that opening. Once we are through, it isn't far to the mouth of the canyon. That is where the fun begins," Dorje said rather grimly.

There was snow along the ridge, and there were thick layers of ice on granite walls on each side of the crack in the ridge.

"This is rather like threading a needle," Jeff thought to himself as he wiped the sweat from his forehead with the back of his hand.

This was certainly a white-knuckle experience for Jeff, but nothing like what lay ahead.

There was tension inside the helicopter. Once on the other side of the ridge, Dorje began to lose altitude. After several minutes, he announced they were nearing the mouth of the canyon. Look as they would, all they could see were solid masses of granite. When it seemed they were about to crash headlong into the side of a mountain, Dorje made a sharp turn to the right. Dead ahead was the very narrow opening to the canyon.

"Can we make that," was Jeff's panicked thought as Dorje skillfully maneuvered the helicopter through.

What began then was a turning, up and down flight in a narrow, deep, winding trench of granite. In places, the walls were so close it seemed the blades would strike against them. There was not the slightest bit of room for error. They all knew Himalayan weather could change in minutes. If they should run into a heavy mist or clouds forced down from the high peaks by wind, they would not stand a chance. There was no turning back.

The world both inside and outside the cabin seemed to be moving in slow motion. After they had been in the canyon for what seemed to be a lifetime, Dorje broke the silence. They had entered the upper part of the canyon. This proved to be the fairly straight part of the whole flight.

"That steep wall in front of us—that's the end of the canyon, at least the part we can fly in. I've got to gain enough altitude to get us over. It may look easy," he continued, "but it can be really tricky. There tends to be much unstable air that swirls around at its base. I think, because the weather is so calm, we should not have too rough a ride, but you can never tell. Therefore, be ready, just in case."

Dorje wasn't kidding about having to gain altitude. The helicopter immediately shot up at such a fast rate it made both Jeff and his parents gasp with fright. For a few minutes, the air was smooth, but the closer they came to the wall, the more turbulent it became and the rougher their ride. At one point, it became so rough all but Dorje grabbed onto their seats for extra support. A great updraft of air swished them up as though lending a much-needed push, and they were up and over the thin ribbon of wall.

Once they were safely on the other side, Dorje let out a sudden whoop of joy and said, "Now, it is all downhill." Gently, like a leaf falling in the wind, they tumbled down. Everyone began to relax, and the tension vanished.

"It won't be long now," Dorje said, pointing his finger. "Over there, beyond the lower of those two ridges, there is our valley. We won't land there, but where we will land is not very far from the entrance. It is the same spot where the helicopters land when they bring in supplies or pick someone up who has to leave the valley."

"Is there anyone at the landing site?" Jeff asked.

"Yes, there are always at least two men who stay there. Now, Jeff," he said while reaching inside his coat and pulling out a long, white scarf, "when I tell you, you are to hold this scarf out your window so it can be seen from the ground. That is the signal we have to give to be able to land. Remember, this helicopter carries the markings of the Chinese army, and I certainly do not want to be mistaken for one of them."

He came in fairly high over a tree-covered hill. On the other side they saw a small clearing. They were still high above the spot when Dorje began to lose altitude in a series of slow, tight circles.

"Hold the scarf out the window," he said to Jeff when they were low enough that it could easily be seen from the ground. "When I see someone standing in the middle of the clearing and waving a scarf in the air, we can land."

"There," shouted Jeff excitedly, "someone has just run to the center of the clearing, and he's waving a white scarf."

"I see him," answered Dorje, smiling. "Now, it's good old Mother Earth for us."

Turning to his parents, Jeff gave them the thumbs up signal, and they began to laugh.

As they climbed down from the helicopter, even Dorje admitted solid earth had never felt so good.

Jeff and his parents spent several weeks in the valley. After they had been there a few days, Bajay returned with the horses and to the heartfelt thanks of the three Thorntons for all the help he had provided. Dorje's parents treated Jeff's parents like honored guests, as did the rest of the friendly people living in the valley. They spent most of the time together riding, fishing, hiking, and loved every minute of it. Sometimes, Dorje would go with them.

Late one afternoon, Jeff and his parents were sitting on the bank of the stream where Jeff had discovered the yeti footprint. Jeff gave them an account of what he had seen. He told them the story Dorje had related about how his father and his friends found this beautiful valley, plus how the yetis sill look after them today.

Jeff's parents said they would tell him their story—but not now. They did say even though Colonel Chin was an evil, but very intelligent man, he knew nothing about chemistry. Jeff's father, with a big smile on his face, said that what they had been working on at the monastery would probably not even harm an ant.

One evening while eating, Dorje's father said to them, "It is time," he began movingly, "for the three of you to return to your home. All of the arrangements have been taken care of. Your government has been notified, and they will contact you when you arrive. You will fly from here in an Indian army helicopter day after tomorrow to a place in India. From there, you will be flown by plane to New Delhi and then home. We...all of us here in this valley...will miss you. Some day we hope you will return. You will always be welcome," he ended with true warmth in his voice.

On that last day, Dorje went with them to visit and thank the people of the valley. He took Hercules for a short ride by himself. When he returned, he could not hide the tears in his eyes, and he did not even try.

As they were getting ready to leave, Jeff asked Dorje about Colonel Chin. "Will he try to kidnap my parents again?"

"I don't think you have anything to worry about," he answered reassuringly, "because it has been reported through certain channels to the Chinese government about Colonel Chin's activities and ambitions. Through these same channels, the crash of a helicopter with Chinese markings was reported. The report stated the crash occurred on the side of a mountain just over the border in India. Three bodies were found in the wreckage."

When they had said goodbye, both Jeff and Dorje knew they had become as close as two friends could. It made things much easier when Dorje told Jeff they would see each other again.

Things went quickly and smoothly, and before they knew it, they were boarding the plane in New Delhi for the flight home. Even though they were excited, they were so exhausted. They fell asleep almost as soon as the jet was airborne. The last thoughts Jeff had before drifting off to sleep were of Trudy and all he had to tell her.

TATE PUBLISHING & *Enterprises*

Tate Publishing is commited to excellence in the publishing industry. Our staff of highly trained professionals, including editors, graphic designers, and marketing personnel, work together to produce the very finest books available. The company reflects the philosophy established by the founders, based on Psalms 68:11,

"THE LORD GAVE THE WORD AND GREAT WAS THE COMPANY OF THOSE WHO PUBLISHED IT."

If you would like further information, please call
1.888.361.9473
or visit our website
www.tatepublishing.com

TATE PUBLISHING & *Enterprises*, LLC
127 E. Trade Center Terrace
Mustang, Oklahoma 73064 USA